Gideon John Tucker

Legends of the Netherlands

Gideon John Tucker

Legends of the Netherlands

ISBN/EAN: 9783337390891

Printed in Europe, USA, Canada, Australia, Japan

Cover: Foto ©Andreas Hilbeck / pixelio.de

More available books at **www.hansebooks.com**

LEGENDS

OF THE

NETHERLANDS

TO WHICH ARE ADDED SOME

LEGENDS OF MANHATTAN ISLAND.

BY

GIDEON J. TUCKER, A.M., LL.D.

———

Brave old Fatherland! over the sea
Thy distant descendants dwell proudly on thee!
Thy homely virtues, thy love for toil
Thy sons have transplanted to other soil,
And they will maintain, wherever they be,
Religion tolerant, and Government free.

———

PRINTED FOR THE AUTHOR BY
THE CONCORD COÖPERATIVE PRINTING COMPANY
———
NEW YORK, 1892.

These Volkslieds of our forefathers I dedicate to the millions of native born Americans who are descended from Holland Dutch ancestry.

GIDEON J. TUCKER.

July, 1892.

THE TECTOSAGES.

B. C. 390—280.

Who shall sing of the Tectosages,
　　Sons of marshy Belgian soil,
Foremost where the battle rages,
　　Seeking conquest, loving spoil?
Gaul has seen their roving legions,
　　Of resistance making mock,
Occupy her choicest regions,
　　Settling in fair Languedoc.

Not yet are their wanderings ended,
　　Down the Danube pour their hordes,
Macedonia, undefended,
　　Heeds their summons, dreads their swords.
Swim they next the deep Bosphorus,
　　Timid Asia fears the fray,
Hears their wild, barbaric chorus,
　　Yields to their imperious sway.

Famed for valorous doings, no man
  Braves the Belgic lion's whelp,
Pyrrhus leads them 'gainst the Roman,
  Carthage buys their willing help:
Through dark scenes of blood and pillage,
  Conflict brave and plunder base,
Ruined town and smoking village,
  Early history marks their trace.

Theirs is Toulouse, heaped with treasure,
  Spoils of Asia and Greece,
Gold and silver beyond measure,
  Prize of war and pride of peace :
When her foe his victim swallowed,
  And the town betrayed and sold,
Fearful was the curse that followed
  On Tolosa's stolen gold.

Sing the tale of the Tectosages,
  Sing their fierce, heroic deeds,
Dimly note we, through the ages,
  Their achievements and their greeds :

Murder–doing, plunder–hoarding,
  Long forgot their land of birth,
All we know is their marauding,
  Carried over half the earth.

CIVILIS STANDING ON THE BROKEN BRIDGE.

A. D. 70.

The brave Batavians, children of the sea,
  Long waged their fierce rebellion against
    Rome,
Wild as their tempests, as their waters free,
  Though bleak and bare the dunes they
    called their home :
Once Rome's best soldiers; all allegiance
    spurned,
Now their tried arms were 'gainst her
    eagles turned.

Civilis, hater of the foreign yoke,
  Led forth his countrymen on flood and
    field,
And oft the power of the legions broke,
  And taught the stubborn Romans first to
    yield ;
And, though the ocean rose o'er Betuwe,
The billows spared the children of the
    sea.

His fleet the Consul Cerealis lost,
  The Meuse the captured Roman galleys
      bore,
Gay with their painted sails, and the great
    host
  Of armed barbarians lined the further
      shore ;
To these the Consul's sacred heralds come
To bring Civilis overtures from Rome.

A wooden bridge a sluice's waters spanned,
  They broke it, at the middle of the tide,
Civilis stood upon the hither end,
  And Cerealis on the farther side,
And the debate began with earnest tongue,
For chains or freedom on its issue hung.

The veil, which History's uplifted hand
  Has partly raised, that moment darkly fell.
How fared it with Civilis and his land ?
  No mortal tongue or pen shall ever tell!
Yet, through long centuries, which inter-
    vene,
Civilis, standing on that bridge, is seen.

Wars, waged for conquest, dynasty or creed,
   Have cursed men since their records first
      begin;
Those only can be reckoned just indeed,
   Fought on behalf of country, home and
      kin :
Known to all peoples, languages and lands,
Upon that broken bridge Civilis stands.

A conqueror rears a statue or a shaft,
   A tyrant revels amid venal praise,
The selfish servitors of force and craft
   Their effigies and trophies vainly raise:
The patriot hero lives from age to age,
Immortal, glorious, on History's page.

AUGUSTUS CARAUSIUS.

IN THE THIRD CENTURY.

Dedicate1 to his historian, Gen. J. Watts De Peyster.

Stormy and strong are the winds that howl
    through the British Channel,
Rough and threatening the waves that roll
    in the Northern Ocean,
There the Hollander rocks like a child in a
    cradle,
There with the sea and the storm he wages
    eternal conflict.

Famed for his courage and skill was the
    Dutch sailor, Carausius,
Baseborn, they said, but young, and of
    strength and beauty Godlike,
None so skillful as he, guiding his rudder
    midst tempests,
None so terribly fierce on the wet decks of a
    sea fight.

Reigned at Rome the Emperor, mighty Au-
gustus Maximian,
Lord of the Western world: thus spoke he
to Carausius—
"Pirates and corsairs trouble the coasts of
Gaul and of Britain,
Sweep them clean and quiet; I create thee
Thalassiarch."

Forth o'er the Northern Ocean poured the
ships of the Dutchman,
Swept it clean and quiet, drowned the hosts
of sea robbers,
Sailed through the British Seas down to the
Bay of Biscay,
Scourged the Danes and the Northmen,
scourged the plundering Bretons.

High on Carausius' mast there floated the
white-horse banner,
Bright on his shield a ship seemed sailing
lone on the ocean

Thus did Carausius win the sacred name of
    Augustus:
Everywhere over the waters brooded the
    peace of Augustus.

From Rome there came the tardy praise and
    thanks of the Senate;
The Emperor gave to the sailor the title and
    honors of sovereign;
Still extant are the medals, bearing the proud
    inscriptions,
Showing the lord of the seas become the
    monarch of Britain.

But the tyrants at Rome as sudden revoked
    their favor,
Waged a war with Carausius everywhere in
    Armorica;
Back he hasted to Holland, overthrew
    Rome's legions,
Defeated on sea and land the Cæsar Con-
    stantius Chlorus.

Then he died at York, struck by Alectus'
    dagger,
Then his realm fell to pieces, and the fierce
    Romans regained it;
Pirates again on the seas,—robbery, violence,
    murder,—
All attested the loss of the Dutch Augustus
    Carausius.

FRIESLAND AND ZEELAND.

In the Ninth Century.

The Counts of Holland had many a fief,
  Held of the Kaiser by feudal law,
But Friesland knew no imperial chief,
  And free was the sceptre her ruler bore.

The Emperor gave to the roving Danes
  The land of Friesland, without a right,
But Friesland's sons retook the domains
  And overcame the heathen in fight.

And, beside the forest of Wanda, naught
  Of the land of Zeeland the Kaiser held ;
For faith and freedom the Zeelanders fought
  Till Danish rule was at last expelled.

And nowhere was known, since the world
    began,
  A people stronger or rulers more weak,
For in Friesland and Zeeland every man
  Might think and reason and write and
    speak.

HOW THE BISHOP SAVED UTRECHT.

A. D. 1137.

Utrecht's Bishop demanded Friesland
    As his own province, subject and liege,
Count Theodore did the claim withstand,
    And shut up Utrecht with sudden siege.

Closer and closer the lines were pressed,
    Right Reverend Heribert's garrison
       quailed,
Not even his prayers, though he prayed at
    his best,
    Nor fastings, processions nor relics
       availed.

The day had come for the final assault,
    The Hollanders massed for mounting the
       wall,
Unless there be somewhere a falter, or fault,
    Old Utrecht is surely about to fall!

Lo, the city's portal is opening itself:
  What is issuing forth—an armed sortie?
The Ritterband fighters for plunder and
    pelf
  Recoil astounded at what they see.

In full canonicals, mitre and gown,
  Escorted by priest and by alcolyte,
With monks in black robe and friars in
    brown,
  And crosiers and crosses paraded in sight,

With solemn ritual and anthem loud,
  With a bearing free from alarm or doubt,
With a lofty mien and attitude proud,
  The Bishop of Utrecht passes out.

That lighted candle, full well they know,
  An excommunication portends;
The soldiers away their weapons throw,
  The Bishop advances—resistance ends.

Spiritual power the victory gains,
  Banners droop and the shoutings still,
Psalmody stifles the warlike strains,
  And his enemies bow to the Bishop's will.

The penitent Count is humbly shriven,
  Of Utrecht and Friesland rests Heribert
    lord ;
The realm is saved that devotion had given ;
  So does the crosier subdue the sword.

COUNT WILLEM'S CRUSADE.

A. D. 1218.

Count Willem of Holland had piously vowed
    To cross his sword with the Paynim afar ;
With stalwart yeomen and cavaliers proud,
    In twelve great ships he sailed for the
      war.

Long they tossed on the heaving sea,
    Those brave Dutch sailors who feared for
      naught,
And a weary man was Willem, when he
    One day cast anchor in Lisbon port.

"O, tarry and help!" cried the Portuguese
    King,
    "For the cursed followers of false Ma-
      hound
Have seized Alczar, and they force us to
    bring
    A tribute of Christian captives bound."

Down from their vessels, with sword in hand,
   The Dutchmen leaped, and retook Alczar,
The slaves were restored to the grateful land,
   And Willem sailed for the distant war.

Then steered he East, for the cross to fight,
   Where the swelling floods of the Nile come
      down,
Where shone the domes and minarets bright
   O'er the walls of Damietta town.

Girt was that city with lofty towers,
   Strong and brave were the men within;
The foul fiend summoned his utmost powers
   To baffle the Christians' attempt to win.

Demoniac faces mock from the wall,
   Sounds as from Hell break the calm of
      night,
Fiendish enchantments the Christians ap-
      pal,
   And devils seize on the fallen in fight.

Across the channel was stretched and tied
   To the opposite bank a great iron chain,
Below it the good Dutch ships could ride,
   But the upper river they could not gain.

The chain is severed—the towers fall!
   'Twas the Haarlem men the attack began;
The Dutchmen clamber the bristling wall,
   'Twas Haarlem burghers who led the van!

The turbaned foemen sullenly yield,
   The suppliant city is at his feet,
Impatient Willem lays by his shield
   And hurries his booty aboard the fleet.

"Ho, for our homes by the Northern Sea!
   We have fought the fight and have kept
     our vows;
We have proven our faith and our chivalry—
   Hasten, and homeward turn our prows."

Home they come with their marvellous tales,
  Tales which a thousand additions en-
    hance,
Beside Count Willem's crusade pales
  The strangest story of old romance.

And Haarlem—old Haarlem—still keeps the
    day
  Whereon that Paynim city was won,
And honors the fallen crusaders who lay
  Where their bones were bleached by the
    torrid sun.

Then Willem, good Willem, to Middelburgh
    gave
  A charter which rendered her citizens free:
He rests in a blessed and honored grave;—
  God send us others as worthy as he!

THE COUNTESS JANE.

A. D. 1223.

I tell the tale of a frightful deed,
  Of a hapless sire by his daughter slain,
Slain for a wicked woman's greed—
  The terrible crime of the Countess Jane.

Baldwin, Emperor, lord of the East,
  Escaped from the wild Bulgarian horde,
Hoping to find a refuge at least,
  All things lost but his honor and sword,

Back to Flanders returned, to find
  His place usurped and his claims decried,
For his daughter Jane, with words unkind,
  His very person and face denied.

"Shameless imposter, who mocks the dead,
  Hence to a prison and scaffold!" she cried,
"For he, who was of this state the head,
  In far Bulgarian deserts died."

But Flanders spoke with a single voice,
  "A welcome home to our feudal lord!
We see our Count, and we all rejoice
  To pledge to him every loyal sword!"

The wicked Countess besought the aid,
  Of the King of France, her throne to gain,
And Louis promptly the call obeyed,
  And his knights brought back the haugh-
    ty Jane.

Her husband lies in the Louvre tower,
  Her father died by the headsman's hand,
The Countess sits in her lonely bower
  And rules, with an iron rule, the land.

But long as Merit must yield to Fate,
  And long as sin brings lasting shame,
The bard will sing and the scribe relate
  The terrible crime of the Countess Jane.

GUY DAMPIERRE AND HIS DAUGH-TER.

A. D. 1300.

When the countship of Flanders was held by
    Guy Dampierre,
He sought to wed his daughter to the
    English monarch's heir ;
Phillipina was a damsel quite worthy of a
    prince,
For beauty none surpassed her then and
    none exceed her since ;
But because the French King Philip was
    Flanders' feudal lord,
The marriage was suspended to await his
    royal word.

" Far be it from me to insist upon my feudal
    right,
By which I could forbid the bans, and
    work ye such despite,

But, because I am godfather to such a
    charming maid,
I fain would see and bless her in her bridal
    robes arrayed;
So, pay me now the visit I so many years
    have sought,
See Paris and its splendors and the pleasures
    of my court."

They trusted the false monarch : he got them
    in his power,
He locked them safe in dungeons in the
    famous Louvre tower,
And vainly did Pope Benedict, with all the
    world, protest,
Since Philip only answered all remon-
    strance with a jest ;
So the beauteous Phillipina, of the Vlaen-
    derland the pride,
Perhaps from long imprisonment, perhaps
    by poison, died.

THE CIVIL WAR OF THE CODS AND THE HOOKS.

A. D. 1300—1500.

The banquet in the town hall had been set,
Nobles and citizens together met ;
The feast had reached the phase of drink
    and toast,
When some vain lordling made a wanton
    boast—
" We nobles eat you commoners as we wish.
You are the bait, and we the swallowing
    fish ! "
A burgher blurted forth—" 'tis very odd,
The baited hook so often takes the cod ! "
The quick retort awoke responsive sound,
And with loud echo went the laugh around.

The names of factions rise from feud or feast,
Some happy answer, or some sneering jest,
And for two centuries in Holland raged
The war this festive play of words presaged.

The commune men deliberately took
From their response the vaunting name of
    Hook,
While those who would a prouder station
    claim
In the Cod found an emblematic name;
And ere the warfare ended, many a plain
Was cursed and cumbered with red heaps of
    slain.

THE BATTLE OF COURTRAI.

A. D. 1302.

O fearful was the slaughter at the battle of
    Courtrai,
When before our Flemish burghers the
    knights of France gave way,
When was gathered in the harvest of hate
    that had been sown,
And full revenge was taken on the tyrant
    Chatillon.

Their Queen against our people maintained
    a bitter spite,
To her alone belongs the provocation of that
    fight;
As if she had the purpose our manhood to
    arouse,
She said, "Kill me these Flemish boars, and
    do not spare the sows!"

When she came to visit Flanders, the jewels,
    silks and gold,
Worn by our dames, revealed to her a mine
    of wealth untold,
Inflamed by ire and jealousy she sneered a
    royal sneer—
"I thought myself the only Queen; I see six
    hundred here!"

And Chatillon, our Governor, with our poor
    town was wroth,
And decreed that every workman from his
    wages pay one-fourth;
And when Philippe commanded that certain
    goods be made,
He punished those who made them for clam-
    oring to be paid.

Our commune he abolished, and denied our
    burgher right;
Then good old Pieter Koning roused our
    people to the fight—

"Awake, brave Bruges, haste and seize thy
    targe, and torch, and brand,
For there's a bloody rising throughout the
    Vlaenderland!"

To Courtrai the flower of French chivalry
    was sent,
To Courtrai we burghers marched—our motto
    "Scilt en vriendt!"
At Courtrai on that July day we slaughter-
    ed them like curs,
And hung up, as our trophies, four thousand
    gilded spurs.

O patriot town of Bruges, which waited not
    for Ghent!
Thine was the stern rebuke that to that
    wicked Queen was sent!
Thy fierce revolt had wakened up but slow-
    ly through the land,
But when it struck, the blow was dealt as
    with an iron hand!

Philippe lost all his Barons upon that fate-
    ful day,
And the Holy Father cursed him, and the
    Bishops fell away;
And Courtrai taught a lesson worth the pon-
    dering of a King—
Beware how you disturb our hives, for work-
    ing bees can sting!

THE BURNING ALIVE OF THE KNIGHTS TEMPLAR.

AT PARIS, A. D. 1314.

Through the Christian realms there went
    forth the cry,
  " The accursed Paynim bear rule and sway
In the Holy Land where our Lord did die,
    O'er the sepulchre where his body lay; —
The Moslem are trampling our sacred things;
Arouse, Oh nations, and arm, Oh Kings!"

From cot and castle, from bourg and court,
    Swarmed forth crusaders, pious and brave,
By myriads they marched, and prayed and
    fought,
  The Land of the Cross to redeem and save;
And they won back by valor the sacred sod,
Where Solomon builded the temple of God.

Where the crucified Saviour's body had lain
  The Templar Knights were guards of the
    tomb,
Till the hosts of the Moslem prevailed again,
  And the Christian Kingdom sank to its
    doom ;
For it seemed good in the sight of the Lord
That the land should revert to the Infidel
    horde.

The Templar Knights, from their Palestine
    driven,
  Brought back their scanty and shattered
    bands ;
Their prayers the poor to their aid had given,
  The rich had given them manors and lands;
And great and wealthy their Order became
And hate and envy attended its fame.

For Europe was suffering, and gaunt with,
    despair,
  With greed and ambition its rulers were
    drunk,

Its towns were in ruins, its acres were bare,
  And all were in want but the Jew and the
     monk ;
So the Pope and the King, in the depth of
    their need,
To divide the spoil of the Templars agreed.

Horrible things to their charge were brought,
  Sorcery, sodomy, heresies,
Fiendish rites by the demons taught,
  Self-absolution, and blasphemies :
And Clement and Philip their conscience ap-
    peased,
By having both Templars and treasure
    seized.

Crippled and crushed, from their torture
    den,
  With broken joint and dismembered frame,
Twisted and racked out of shape of men,
  Before the tribunal the Templars came,

Revoking what paltry and shameful lies
Were wrung from their lips by their ag-
    onies.

The sickening tale of their awful doom,
    Dragged by the score to a death of fire,
Is told by the scribe of a rare old tome
    Who saw the last of the Templars expire:
With them died Knighthood, its romance
      and pride ;
With them the age of the Crusades died.

When the Grand Master the charges repelled,
    And made to the Holy Father appeal,
King Philip his manly protest quelled
    And hastened his fiery fate to seal :
The Parliament gardens were wide and fair,
And he burned the Master to ashes there.

From the seething flames came a summons
    loud,
    In the voice of the sufferer, Jacques
    Molay—

" Ho, Pontiff the mighty, ho, King the proud,
  I summon ye both, ere a year pass away,
For avarice, cruelty, crime, to atone.
Meet me, and answer, before God's throne!"

Then Philip's sister and his wicked Queen
  Both died, and their deaths were a mys-
    tery ;
Then the awful shame of his daughters was
    seen ;
  Then, suddenly, Philip himself did die ;
And Clement's abandoned corpse long lay
Unburied;—all, ere a year passed away !

THE EXILE OF PIETER DU BOIS FROM GHENT.

A. D. 1386.

"The Duke has pardoned our noble Ghent,
　He will not fail of his knightly word;
Faith with the town is surely meant;
　'Tis won by treaty, and not by sword."

To Pieter Du Bois thus Atreman spake;
　Gallantly each had fought for the town,
Vainly, for Ghent must submission make,
　And the great city was quieted down.

"For me," said Pieter, "I trust him not;
　Pardon is naught but a spoken word;
The Duke our warfare has not forgot;
　Commons never can trust a lord.

" I am a man of but lowly birth,
  Freely for Ghent have I risked my life ;
Dear to me is this spot of earth,
  Dearer are freedom, and child, and wife.

" I will go to the Council straight,
  My frank request it will not withstand,
I will ask for an exile's fate,
  For leave to dwell in a foreign land."

So Pieter sailed to a stranger shore,
  Safely escaping with life and limb,
His kin, his goods, his fortune he bore ;
  But Atreman tarried—they murdered
    him !

THE LORDS OF MAESTRICHT.

A. D. 1400.

The Liege Bishop and the Duke of Brabant
    Together have governed our Maestricht
    town,
Both can be rulers, but one of them can't,
    They have two heads, but they wear but
    one crown.
        For one lord is no lord,
        And two lords but one lord.
        Een heer—geen heer,
        Twen heeren—een heer!

When the Bishop is absent, the Duke can-
    not act,
    When the Duke is away, the Bishop is
    naught,
If perchance the two an agreement have
    lacked,
    (As is often the case), confusion is wrought.

For one lord is no lord,
And two lords but one lord.
Een heer—geen heer,
Twen heeren—een heer!

HOW ARNOLD BEILING DIED.

A. D. 1424.

Brave old Arnold Beiling!
  My very soul is stirred,
As I read in ancient story,
  How he kept his plighted word.

The Hooks had been besieging
  The old Schoonhoven Fort,
Defended by some nobles,
  And some of the baser sort;

And when at last it yielded,
  Though hot from recent strife,
The nobles spared the nobles,
  And granted grace and life.

Chief of the burgher party,
  Arnold, they would not spare;
The sins of his associates,
  Arnold alone must bear;

And him alone their vengeance
  Would of his life deprive,
And they passed the dreadful sentence
  To bury him alive.

Pale, but with resolution,
  He asked for brief delay,
To embrace his friends and kindred,
  Until a certain day.

Such the man's faith and courage
  That they allowed him free,
For they knew his promise sacred,
  Without a surety.

Upon the day appointed,
  Before the sun was high,
Calmly returned old Arnold,
  And yielded him to die.

Naught but a simple burgher,
  Without a titled name,
Yet where is King or noble
  But would envy him his fame?

THE DAYS OF THE DUKES OF BURGUNDY.

A. D. 1419—1477.

In the days of Philip and Charles the Bold,
Such extravagance reigned as cannot be told.
Rich were the Netherlands, reckless were
  they,
And their flaunt of magnificence shamed the
  day:
With a profligate suite and a crowded court,
Days given to feastings and nights to sport,
A gorgeous display within palace walls,
Of jewels, and costumes, and jousts and balls,
Where a thousand fashions the sovereign
  would set,
And courtiers follow, though crippled with
  debt.
When Philip was sick, and his head must
  shave,
An order that all must be shaven, he gave,
And five hundred noblemen, little and big,
Employed each a barber, and bought each a
  wig.

It was boasted that no other ruler could
    wring
From his people an income befitting a King.
Did the Duke visit Paris? all Paris, agape,
Was crazed o'er his costumes and charmed
    with his shape :
His horses, his table, his equipage fine,
Court ladies decided to be just divine.
He seemed, as by the old scribe 'tis ex-
    pressed,
Of an inexhaustible treasure possessed.

How did the realm such expenses bear?
How did the commoner classes fare?
The people were laboring with right good
    wills;
The winds turned the sails of a thousand
    mills;
Each acre, reclaimed from the Northern
    Sea,
Was tilled with a patient industry;
And myriads of cattle rich pastures found
On the waving fields of the rescued ground,

The forges roared and the ship yards rang,
And with tireless humming the cloth looms
      sang;
A thousand trade ships explored every sea,
And the land was as busy as it could be.
Each burgher good in the Netherlands
Worked, honest and well, with his head and
      hands,
And, living on Industry's well-earned wage,
Was a notable man in that idle Age.

The rest of Europe was suffering and sad,
But each Dutchman an air of jollity had,
The rest of Europe was wretched and poor,
But plenty sat at each Dutchman's door;
The rest of Europe was ruled by the sword
Of the tyrant King, or the robber lord;
And the plains of Europe scant harvests
      could yield,
For the peasants were swept to the battle
      field,
(Where knights, clad in armor from heel to
      crown,
Courageously rode naked yeomen down;)

And whatever the laboring hind might make
The gentry, by right of their birth, might
    take :
But the Dutchman was ruled by his equals
    and mates,
And his laws were made by his own Estates.

The rest of Europe had little of skill,
For the commons were taught but to ravage
    and kill,
And man upon man heaped unuttered woes,
Who no quarrel had with his so-called foes.
The rest of Europe knew little of art,
Of a building plan or a mariner's chart;
While the Dutchman reared church and pal-
    ace and hall,
With pinnacle, tower and steeple tall,
Whose lofty arches and porticoes wide,
Proved the architect's skill and the citizens'
    pride ;
And dykes, and bridges, and roads and
    canals,
And high and defiant city walls.

With impartial palette the Dutchman could
    paint
The revel of boor or the rapture of saint,
And his matchless pictures will always be
    found
Wherever the lovers of art abound.

While the rest of Europe was filled with
    alarm,
The Dutchman remained without fear of
    harm ;
While the rest of Europe was chilled by the
    storm,
The Dutchman's houses were dry and warm;
While the rest of Europe in rags was clad,
The Dutchman furs and thick woolens had ;
While the rest of Europe was scanty of food,
The Dutchman had plenty, both cheap and
    good ;
The German feasted on hogs and dried geese,
The Englishman fattened on tripe and cheese,
The Spaniard swaggered on garlic and bread,
The Italian upon maccaroni was fed,

But the Dutchman, who sailed the ocean
    through,
All manner of fish from its bosom drew,
And on the canals one had very poor luck,
Who could not for dinner have a roast duck.
With rabbits his barrenest sandhills teemed,
And clouds of wild fowl in inlets screamed ;
Dutch beeves were famous for size and fat,
And pigeons in clouds upon rooftrees sat :
And every root and fruit that was known,
Each kitchen garden could call its own.
While the rest of Europe was empty and
    starved,
The Dutchman his ample dinner carved,
Nor failed to bring, from the banks of the
    Rhine,
Or Burgundy hill sides, the choicest of wine.

True, there were outrages weighty and sad,
Which the Dutch from the Dukes of Bur-
    gundy had.
The money drain of those feudal chiefs,
To their thrifty souls were perpetual griefs ;

But the obstinate burghers rarely paid
Their taxes unless some grievance was
    stayed ;
More independent in their walled towns,
Than Philip or Charles, who wore ducal
    crowns.
Did the prince want cash ? the cash he could
    find,
The moment some charter or franchise was
    signed,
And glad were the Dukes to barter such
    grants,
For means to tide over their frequent wants;
And shrewd and wise in their peaceful might
Were the burghers, who cheaper could buy
    than fight.
So dealt they with Philip and Charles the
    Bold,
And won their freedom by patience and gold.

HOW BURGUNDY GOT LUXEM-
BOURG.

A. D. 1462.

Said Louis the King to the Seigneur Chinay,
" Your Duke of Bourgogne gives me trouble
 each day,
In what does he differ from other lords
That he vexes my patience with peevish
 words ?
Is he made of other metal, that he
Should thus presume with impunity ? "

Said the Seigneur Chinay to Louis the King,
" The Duke *is* a very different thing
From the holiday lords who in swarms re-
 sort
To your Royal Majesty's gilded court ;
Of another metal he surely is made,
For of Kings of France he was never afraid.

" There was a desperate day, long since,
When a French King exiled his son, a Prince,

And a certain Duke the exile received,
His cause sustained and his state retrieved ;
That Duke could none but my master be,
And that exiled Prince was—Your Majesty !"

The wise King heeded the bold rebuke,
And Luxembourg gave to his friend, the
    Duke.

CHARLES OF GUELDERLAND.

A. D. 1500.

Old Duke Arnold of Guelderland,
With a palsied tongue and a shaking hand,
Sold to Burgundy's Duke his crown,—
But the money agreed on was not paid down.
Duke Arnold died without getting the cash,
Which showed his bargain with Burgundy
    rash ;
But Burgundy, doffing his gauntlets and
    helm,
Imperial homage did for the realm.

The usurper, further pursuing his game,
Bought the Berg and Juliers outlawed claim,
And, with a force they could not withstand,
Subjected the freemen of Guelderland.
But soon he lay in a gory bed,
And his daughter Mary reigned in his stead ;
And Mary confirmed all the charters old,
For love of the people, or gift of their gold,

And new ones granted to town and state,
That their vested rights might never abate.
But Mary fell from her horse and died,
So fell the Burgundy power and pride!
And Philip was Count of Holland, and he
Also would Duke of Guelderland be.

Old Duke Arnold a grandson had left,
Who of his dukedom appeared bereft,
But, brave as a lion and shrewd as a fox,
Charles Van Egmond dealt in hard knocks,
Or in subtle craft, as the case might demand,
And soon he was master of Guelderland.
Sad to think of the maimed and dead,
Of the blood so freely, so uselessly shed;
Sad to picture the ruin and waste
The works of labor and art effaced,
The burning town and the murderous field,
The besieged, who slowly to famine yield,
The war on the helpless, the deeds of shame,
Which heroes denominate glory and fame;
The eye grows dim and the heart beats with
        pain,
In reviewing these horrors over again.

And all these miseries, losses and fears,
The land endured for full fifty years.
Little of mercy had Charles, be sure,
For starving peasant and homeless boor,
For power and rank in that hapless time
Were the prizes of cruelty, craft and crime.
So, with the aid of Frenchmen and Dane,
He reddened full many a battle plain,
With his people's blood, for what he could
    call
His rights—though *they* had no rights at
    all.

At Amsterdam's gates his banners flew
And seas and rivers his cruisers knew,
On ocean and land he made equal war,
'Gainst the Spanish king and the emperor,
(For Philip the Count, in his turn, was dead,
And Carlos reigned in his father's stead:)
Friesland he took with his own good sword,
And Groeningen acknowledged him lord,
And Friedrich, Bishop of Utrecht, his friend,
Both carnal and spiritual aid could lend.

Next, being by popular feeling so backed,
The Hague he captured and terribly sacked,
And Charles Van Egmond of Guelderland
Was the popular idol throughout the land.
But Holland aroused when the Hague was
    burned,
And swiftly and sternly the tide had turned,
And Charles was so soon of his spoils bereft,
That he had nothing but Guelderland left;
Yet half a century wasted in war
Had given him never a hurt nor a scar!

His people, praying that war would cease,
Denied his demands and insisted on peace,
And Guelderland was not slow to refuse
As a ruler the King of France to choose.
Lost were his conquests and fallen his pride,
And with broken heart the veteran died.
Long has his name, or alive or dead,
Been dreaded because of the blood he shed,
Yet Charles, on behalf of Guelderland, broke
The detested weight of a foreign yoke:
And many a monarch with lesser claims
The pen of History a hero names.

CHARLES QUINT IN HIS CRADLE.

A. D. 1500.

Watching a baby's cradle,
  Soft as the summer wind blows
Imperial Margot of Flanders
  Sings, as she watches, and sews.
Who is the infant that slumbers?
  Son of Philip the Fair,
Son of Juana the Foolish,
  'Tis he who lies sleeping there.

Womanlike wonders the watcher
  What his fortunes shall be,
Heir to mighty dominions,
  Continents, isles of the sea;
Grandson of Burgundy's Mary,
  Of Isabella of Spain,
Who shall measure his empire,
  Who can limit his reign?

Soft and blithe is her singing,
　For how can she read his fate?
Know the curse of his power,
　Grieve that it is so great?
Foresee the time when his reason
　Under the load shall have sunk,
Till he flee from human contact,
　To die the death of a monk?

Not in the thoughts of the watcher
　Such dark fancies abide,
But her woman-love for an infant,
　And her Austrian princess' pride:
And in the summer breezes
　Sews she, and sings with glee,
Proud that the boy in the cradle,
　Master of millions must be.

THE SIXTEENTH CENTURY DELUGE.

A. D. 1524.

In the days that we now call the Middle
    Ages
There were no philosophers, very few sages,
But plenty of clericals, soldiers and lords,
Plenty astrologers — all of them frauds.
There were horoscopes cast, and really be-
    lieved in,
Prophecies uttered—to be deceived in;
People then credited all they were told,
Needless to say that they often got sold;
And the strangest deception the histories
    own
As the Sixteenth Century Deluge is known.

A much learned Dutchman, Steffler by name,
Should be handed down to immortal fame.
By investigation this man had found
That the human race would again be drowned,

In the year, as revealed by his magic lore,
Of fifteen hundred and twenty-four.
That the world its peril might understand
The announcement was made known to every
    land,
And all were advised to be wise and wary
For the flood would be due in February.
Nor did he fail of a calculation
To account for the frightful precipitation;
A conjunction of Jupiter, Saturn and Mars
Would be the caper cut out by the stars,
In the sign of the Fishes—the very quarter
To which you would look for plenty of water.

Throughout the Low Countries spread great
    alarm :
What should men do to be saved from harm?
Many proposed bad acquaintance to drop
And betake themselves to some steeple top,
Others began long-deferred repenting,
While others gave themselves to lamenting.
Husbands rejoiced that their wives could not
    swim,
And wives said, " drowning is too good for
    him ! "

And the very few who expressed a doubt
By sneers and reproaches were put to rout.

Yet some there were, unlike the rest,
Who, having some cash they wished to in-
    vest,
And in the delusion taking no stock,
Set coolly to work to shear the whole flock.
For the mass were ready and eager to sell.
And sellers came seeking the buyers, pell-
    mell,
Till the whole population, with terror mad,
Sold out at dead loss almost all they had.

Up went the cost of tarpaulin clothes,
And the price of salted provisions rose ;
Boat builders came into great demand,
And were eagerly sought for on every hand ;
And every craft that could sail or swim
Was engaged for passengers up to the brim.
Even a savage with a rude canoe
Would have been welcomed with much ado.

A revival of knowledge the epoch marks,
For men rediscovered how to build arks.

One, who'd determined he would not drown,
Was a wealthy burgher of Amsterdam town,
One Vandervoort, whose yacht was so great
That he was considered proof against fate;
So filled with comforts and luxuries rare
That Noah's ark could in nothing compare.

January slowly glided along,
One could purchase a village for a mere song;
And careful observers, watching the sky,
Remarked that it was unusually dry.
The deluge would come, people said, that
    was plain,
For the clerk of the weather was storing up
    rain.

February arrived; still the sun shone bright,
But the popular agony rose to its height;
The churches were crowded; all hastened to
    pray,
Except the boat builders, who worked night
    and day.

It was hard to decide which engrossed the
    most cares,
The building of boats or the saying of
    prayers;
Yet, day by day, as the month hurried by,
Perpetual sunshine poured from the sky.

That year was a leap year, the calendar
    says,
And the second month had twenty-nine
    days;
Yet, while all Holland with panic was
    cowed,
Not one of the twenty-nine brought forth a
    cloud!
Not a drop of rain nor a flake of snow
Fell from the skies to the earth below,
Although the conjunction duly took place,
And clouds of dismay were on Steffler's
    face.

'Twas a blow to the whole soothsayer race,
Who since have been held in deserved dis-
    grace.

But the loss, by the deluge which did not
    come,
Was great to many and total to some ;
For, having invested in boats and arks,
They had nothing now but these useless
    barks,
And multitudes were so wholly bereft
That nothing at all but their lives was left;
But, having escaped from a watery fate,
Like Noah, the Dutchmen could celebrate !

COMMISSIONER SMYTER AT HOORN.

A. D. 1550.

Complaint was made by Father Dirck,
That heresy did foully lurk
Within the town of Hoorn, and so
The Council sought the facts to know,
  And sent Commissioner Smyter.

The burgomaster of the town,
Fearing the mighty Council's frown,
Conceived a most consummate plan
To pacify this dangerous man,
  This same Commissioner Smyter.

The town authorities went out,
Accompanied by the burghers stout,
Encountered him upon his road,
And most respectful courtesy showed,
  Which pleased Commissioner Smyter.

Escorted into Hoorn, they fain
Their worthy guest would entertain,
And long and loud the revel roared,
That night, around the generous board
  Where supped Commissioner Smyter.

At last, when broke the rosy morn,
And the sun's beams the town adorn,
Commissioner Smyter was—well, drunk!
And so was carried to his bunk,
  A tired Commissioner Smyter.

That day came many a sniffling saint
'Gainst other men to make complaint,
But the Commissioner was deep
In the embrace of a sound sleep,
  So slept Commissioner Smyter.

No sooner did they Smyter rouse
Than there began a fresh carouse,
And the Commissioner, full and fed,
Went from his table to his bed,
  So went Commissioner Smyter.

Then each great burgher took his turn,
And gave their guest a chance to learn
Hoorn's hospitality, and he
Passed every night in revelry—
      So did Commissioner Smyter.

And so, for seven mortal days,
Secluded from the common gaze,
He was to all petitions blind,
Nor could the sour complainants find
      The lost Commissioner Smyter.

The day arrived when he must leave,
Whereat the town professed to grieve,
And one more rousing feast was made.
To throw all others in the shade,
      And throw Commissioner Smyter.

When Smyter mounted on his horse,
And tore himself away by force,
They really had to stay him up
To take his parting stirrup-cup,
      So reeled Commissioner Smyter.

Back to the Council Smyter went
Claiming that Hoorn did well repent ;
Such men on pious duties set,
Such godly men, he ne'er had met,
     Said good Commissioner Smyter.

He flat denied to Dirck's own face
That a heretic was in the place;
And as his story well appeared
Old Hoorn was from the charges cleared,
     Thanks to Commissioner Smyter.

CHARLES V. AND THE SIEGE OF METZ.

A. D. 1552.

The Kaiser Karl is mighty and proud,
   The sun on his empire never sets,
And his wrath was high and his vow was
     vowed
   To retake the valiant city of Metz.

Master of Mexico and of Peru,
   Of mountains of treasure beyond the sea,
Yet with empty coffers, he humbly drew
   A loan from Cosmo de Medici.

Splendid and strong, his warlike array
   Had marched, at the Emperor's word, to
     seize
The town which snug by its towers lay,
   Where flew the flag of the Duke of Guise.

And now at the end of seventy days,
  With nearly half of his army slain,
The Kaiser resolves the siege to raise,
  And Metz breathes freely and safe again.

And he defeated! of millions the lord,
  Of slaves and subjects of every hue,
With broken army and broken sword,
  Brave Metz has broken his spirit too.

They say his words are sullen and few,
    That his glance is vague and his brain for-
      gets,
That his family madness came to view
    At his luckless siege of the city of Metz.

They say he intends a last retreat
    From a world whose greatness is dross
      and dust,
That he may his daily prayers repeat
    And sing his anthems at lone St. Just.

VIVENT LES GUEUX!

(Hurrah for the Beggars!)

A. D. 1566.

In Kuitemberg palace the revel was high,
  The Lord Bredenrode gave banquet that
    night,
And what rank could furnish, or treasure
  could buy
Shone brilliant and proud beneath flood-
  ings of light.

And crowds of the reckless young nobles
  were there,
  Who squandered their rentals on tables
    of chance,
And graybeards, who lived an old age of
  despair,
  Since fortune on graybeards looks ever
    askance.

And some were insolvent, and all were in
debt,
Some hated the Regent, some hated the
law,
And some upon change and disturbance
were set,
And all were discordant, impatient and
sore.

Their "Noble's Petition" to Margaret had
prayed
That worship be free from the axe, stake
and cord ;
But Margaret the Regent her answer delayed,
And while she debated, they revelled and
roared.

Then up rose a spokesman; "O, have ye not
learned
What words to the Regent Count Barlaimont said,
When she our petition half welcomed, half
spurned,
And at its bold language blushed suddenly red,

"Then trembled, and stammered, in anger
   and fear,
   And the woman revealed in the puppet of
      state?
Then Barlaimont whispered soft words in
   her ear—
   'These are but as beggars who swarm at
      your gate!'"

Broke forth a loud jeer from the throat of
   each guest;
   "Long life to the Beggars!" was shouted
      and said,
And Brussels at midnight was startled from
   rest,
   And turned every slumbering burgher in
      bed.

"The Beggars!" by that modest name are
   they known,
   With it they will live, and for it they will
      die.
Long life to the Beggars! The King on his
   throne,
   Shall tremble and shrink at that ominous
      cry!

THE THREE ORANGES.

A. D. 1568—1647.

William the Silent was hero and sage,
  The hope of his people, the stay of the
    State,
And, far in advance of his bigoted age,
  His tolerance stamped him deservedly
    great;
The fame of story, the praises of song,
To the martyr prince as of right belong.

Maurice of Orange was selfish and fierce,
  In youth over gay, but in age severe,
No plea for pity his bosom could pierce
  He knew no mercy, and felt no fear:
His vices he vailed 'neath Religion's hood,
And he stained his name with Barneveldt's
    blood.

Frederick Henry, the third of the race,
  The second of William's sons who ruled,
Had ne'er a thought but for power and place,
  And his people alternately bullied and
    fooled.
Thus the great hero shall live in his fame,
With his sons' ill deeds remembered with
  shame.

THE RESCUE OF LEYDEN.

A. D. 1574.

Five months the cruel Spaniards lay
  Beleaguering Leyden's wall,
Within, grim famine held its sway,
  Portending Leyden's fall.
Long since, upon our first alarm,
  We swore to never yield,
While a single famine-wasted arm
  Could any weapon wield.

Starvation was our direst foe—
  No flesh, no fish, no corn—
And weakness checked each earnest blow,
  And made defense forlorn.
Though every house with dead was filled,
  And every street ran blood,
The most who died were hunger-killed,
  Their last words, " Give us food ! "

Our loved ones starved before our eyes—
    Parent, and child, and wife—
More hapless who from hunger dies,
    Than he who falls in strife.
Still no relief : all hope we lose,
    When, in these desperate straits,
Our carrier pigeons bring us news
    From the Council of the States :—

" The dykes are cut, and on the flood
    Two hundred vessels ride ;
To bring you men, and arms, and food,
    They wait but wind and tide."
Still blew the bitter North-east gale,
    And, adverse, swept the coast,
We could discern nor mast nor sail
    Of the relieving host.

Hour after hour that wind prevailed—
    East to North-east its range—
It seemed our promised hope had failed,
    We ne'er should see it change !

At last! the vane has veered around,
   And with tremendous roar,
High surging o'er the level ground
   The ocean's waters pour.

The sea, as though in haste and wrath,
   Sweeps onward in its might,
O'erbears the Spaniards in its path
   Or scatters them in flight;
And, riding on the crested wave,
   A cloud of ships we see
Press onward, Leyden town to save
   In its extremity.

Close to our walls their course is stayed,
   There moor they, safe and free,
For Leyden is an island made,
   Girt with a boundless sea.
Leyden is saved! the rescuing hosts
   Can best the tale relate,
How like we were to pallid ghosts
   Who opened Leyden's gate.

PHILIP'S SOLILOQUY ON HIS BROTHER.

A. D. 1578.

Of England you would be King, Don John,
  And fancied you could betray me!
But I will punish your plotting, Don John,
  For the spy and poisoner obey me.

To England's queen you've made love, Don
    John,
  Your ambition from duty wanders!
And her royal favor to move, Don John,
  You have offered her Spanish Flanders!

A skillful agent I'll send, Don John,
  Who will of a brother bereave me,
And bring your plots to an end, Don John:
  So perish all who deceive me.

SONG OF THE ARTISANS OF ANTWERP.

A. D. 1580.

Free artisans we, who no master own,
   We safely dwell in our guarded town,
We kneel at the foot of no earthly throne,
   And tremble before no tyrant's frown.
Our walls are kept with good watch and
     ward,
   Our schepens' patrol any riot would quell,
And our trained battalions of burgher guard
   Are roused at the tap of the stadt huis bell.

Our craft-guilds settle our labor's price,
   That an equal stipend each workman may
     draw,
The young work under the elders' advice,
   And our hours of labor are fixed by law.

Our votes are our own, our Council to choose,
  And he would be a fool and a dolt,
Who dared our chartered rights to refuse,
  And risk the protest of stern revolt.

Proud are we of each lofty spire,
  Of our city's towers and church's dome,
But prouder far that each can acquire
  A happy spot he can call a home.
The tramp of thousands of hurrying feet,
  Steadily plodding, each morn and night,
Reechoes loud on the busy street,
  And the men who labor can also fight!

THE SPANISH SOLDIER.

(From the Spanish.)

16TH CENTURY.

Long shall the page of history tell of the
    Spanish invader,
Of Netherland cities the scourge, of Nether-
    land coffers the raider;
If Philip delay my pay, he does not forbid
    me to plunder,
And to leave these rebels their wealth would
    be a palpable blunder.

Wo to the high-walled city, when we under-
    take the leaguer;
Wo to the rich, fat burghers, if the spoil be
    scant and meager;
When women and children are shrieking,
    and men for mercy are roaring,
As over the ruined ramparts our disciplined
    phalanx is pouring!

Our captain, Alva, commanding, this stub-
    born people subduing,

Calls each Spanish soldier to rise and be ac-
    tive and doing;

To every Dutchman a foe, to every Dutch
    lass a lover,

With a sword thrust ready for one, and a
    kiss and embrace for the other.

THE FLESHERS OF ANTWERP.

A. D. 1584.

Peaceful feed at Bergen twice ten thousand
  cattle,
While from Antwerp rises fierce the din of
  battle,
Ruddy runs the Scheldt with the stains of
  slaughter,
Parma's Spaniards never give nor ask for
  quarter!

Peaceful feed the oxen, slow their cuds a
  chewing,
While around the town the devil's work is
  doing,
Where each Antwerp artisan is a brave de-
  fender,
Rich men flee, but poor men dare not to surrender.

Peaceful feed the oxen, 'mid the thyme and
daisy,
Mid the growing grasses waxing fat and
lazy,
While their city owners loudly ·are out-
spoken,
As the burgomaster urged the dykes be
broken.

" Why break down the dykes, why set the
sea in motion,
Flooding Bergen pastures with the rushing
ocean ?
All our fattening beeves will for food be
needed,
And the fleshers' protest, shall it be unheed-
ed ?

"Strong are Antwerp's walls, brave are
Antwerp's freemen,
We have need of neither Zeeland's fleet nor
seamen ;

On our good roast viands well our troops
    are faring,   .
And these starving Spaniards must depart
    despairing."

Evil was the hour when, such advice, pre-
    vailing,
Saved the dykes, but filled the proud old
    town with wailing;
Antwerp now has fallen—more's the shame
    and pity!
And proud Parma lords it over field and
    city.

THE TRAGEDY AT DELFT.

(Assassination of William of Orange.)

A. D. 1584.

In the Museum, at the Hague, is seen
   An ancient fire-arm, with two bullets nigh,
You ask, what may these rusty relics mean?
   And the custodian, reverent, makes reply:
"These were the agents of an awful crime,
The tale whereof endureth through all time."

Armed with this weapon, Balthazar Gerard,
   With Philip's ducats heavy in his purse,
Journeyed to Delft from Burgundy afar,
   To earn his title to a nation's curse;
And hid himself beside a certain wall,
Where the grand staircase leaves the din-
     ing hall.

A ringing shot, a fall, a rush, a scream,
  The deadly charge with fatal aim has sped,
Slow trickles down the steps a crimson
    stream,
  William of Orange slumbers with the dead!
These are the bullets through his heart that
    passed,
When Philip gained his mean revenge at
    last.

The title of a martyr he may claim :
  From royal rank and title saved by fate,
Uncrowned he died, and left a patriot's
    name,
  As the first citizen of a free state !
His fame shall flourish until time shall end,
His people's leader and his people's friend!

GRESHAM'S DRAFT ON GENOA.

A. D. 1587.

In London town one Gresham plied his trade,
An English merchant, dealing far and wide
In goods and wares by foreign countries
    made,
And which to English markets he supplied;
A man imbued with patriotic pride,
Shrewd in his dealings, mighty in his wealth;
A school he built, and an exchange beside,
And did what good he could, and not by
    stealth.

At the Escurial lived that cruel King,
Whom history names Philip, King of Spain,
Passing a long bad life in compassing
Ill to his fellow men, and woe and pain
To those he called his subjects; for his brain
Evolved but plans of bigotry and hate,
And he ruled by the sword and rack and
    chain,
Yet failed to subjugate the Holland State.

Now Philip, plotting harm to all the world,
And much enraged by many a sore defeat
Since Holland's flag was on the seas un-
    furled
Resolved upon a great and startling feat,
And caused to be prepared a mighty fleet,
Calling his soldiers out of many lands,
Who at the Spanish ports should quickly
    meet,
And sail for Albion's cliffs and Holland's
    sands.

The old world gave him myriads of brave
    men,
The new world filled his coffers with her gold,
For Spain was mistress of the Indies then,
Her sailors skillful and her soldiers bold,
Her ships equipped with all that they could
    hold
Of provender and engines of fierce war ;
Churchmen had blessed and soothsayers
    foretold
A crowning victory for Philip's star.

Now Genoa was the centre of exchange,
And Philip kept his moneys there in store ;
For, as his varying purposes did change,
France, Flanders, Italy, by turns he tore,
Upheaving Europe to its very core
With civil wars; and for convenience, there
His ready funds were, whether less or more:
And so, it chanced, the merchant Gresham's
    were.

At Cadiz gathered crowds of Spanish craft,
The news through Europe ran with ready
    fame;
Then Gresham drew on Genoa a draft
For all the gold his balances could claim,
Which drained the banks and thwarted
    Philip's game,
For the King's drafts most pitifully fared ;
Six months elapsed before his money came,
And Holland for the struggle was prepared.

QUEEN ELIZABETH ARRAIGNED.

A. D. 1588.

And now has Queen Elizabeth
   Again broke out in rage,
Unbecoming to her station,
   And indecent at her age ;
Of course 'tis her misfortune
   That she is growing old,
But surely 'tis her own fault
   That she becomes a scold.

She sent her lover, Leicester,
   With promise of support,
He brought us many pompous airs,
   But nothing else he brought:
Besure, he had some soldiers,
   But they did the foe no hurt,
For they had the alternative
   To starve, or to desert.

Of the Irish that she sent us,
  She wanted to be rid,
And her swaggering English footmen
  No service to us did:
And of her earls, and lords, and knights,
  Our people sore complain,
For they idled, and they revelled,
  And they sold our towns to Spain.

And all the while Her Majesty,
  Our freedom to betray,
With Philip and with Parma,
  Has been treating day by day:
But all her secret plottings,
  With these congenial mates,
Thanks to our careful watchings,
  Have been known to our Estates.

Now everything, with blasphemy,
  And imprecations high,
This Queen has the audacity
  To publicly deny:

All Europe has her faithlessness
  Most clearly seen and felt,
And her boisterous tongue could never
  Deceive old Barneveldt.

Our envoys, sent to England,
  Her abuse has never spared;
Now the great Armada, coming,
  Finds her but half prepared.
For us, our ships are ready .
  And bide the approaching host,
And, careless of her queenly spite,
  Will guard our Holland coast.

THE SURRENDER OF DEVENTER.

A. D. 1591.

It was old Herman Vandenberg, tipsy and
    vain,
Who held Deventer for Philip of Spain,
And swore that while he a weapon could
    wield,
He never to Maurice the city would yield;
        Yet the City of Deventer
        In ten days did surrender.

For the Spaniard's distrust and the Dutch-
    men's hate
Had placed traitor Herman in desperate
    strait;
The one his fidelity loudly accused,
And to yield to the other he sternly refused;
        Yet the City of Deventer
        In ten days did surrender.

In the breach of the wall, by day and by
    night,
Just able to stand on his legs and fight,
With a glass in one hand, in the other his
    sword,
As brave as a lion and drunk as a lord;
       Yet the City of Deventer
       In ten days did surrender.

And when Vorst Maurice his mines had sunk,
The town surrendered, with old Herman
    drunk;
His vaunts and his threatenings were held in
    disdain,
And Deventer became a Dutch town again.
       For the City of Deventer
       In ten days did surrender.

PHILIP'S HATRED.

A. D. 1598.

Deep and bitter was Philip's hate,
　For those who dwelled in the Netherlands,
Yet—so perverse and stern was fate—
　We despised his power and escaped his
　　hands.

He hated us because we were free,
　Because he never could be our King,
For to him the assertion of liberty
　Was a most unholy, infamous thing.

He hated us for our faith and creed,
　And doomed us all, in his pious wrath,
At the stake to burn, by the axe to bleed,
　To be crushed as an insect in his path.

But not to man does the issue belong
　Of the follies wrought by his hate and
　　pride;
He lived to see us grow great and strong,
　And his heart was broken—and so he died.

THE BATTLE OF TIEL.

A. D. 1600.

Vorst Maurice marched across Brabant,
The Cardinal Archduke to taunt:
Eight hundred men he took along;
The King's troops were two thousand strong,
Victors on many a hard-fought plain,
Veterans of many a long campaign.

In Brabant, on the heath of Tiel,
With the Archduke's force we crossed our
    steel;
Soon, mute in death, their bravest lie,
And the remainder wildly fly,
Spaniards, Italians, Walloons, all,
Before our onset flee or fall.

Though swift did the survivors run,
We captured nearly every one—

Five hundred prisoners in a row,
The value of our victory show;
Vorst Maurice wrote to the Archduke then,
For he was apt with sword or pen:

"There comes report of your commands,
To spare no lives of rebel bands,
And I must know if this be true,
That I may do as you will do."
No word the Archduke deigned reply;
Vorst Maurice bade his prisoners die.

Then we prepared five hundred graves,
And ropes to hang five hundred knaves;
But, in the hour they deemed their last,
Lo! came a courier, speeding fast,
And letters to Vorst Maurice brought,
Wherein was the reply he sought:

"No such an order have I made,
Nor on my soul such sin have laid;

I pray you, then, to ransom hold
Your prisoners, till I send the gold;
And let us now a compact make
That both will quarter give and take."

So Brabant, ruined, plundered, poor,
Must one exaction more endure,
And must a heavy ransom give,
For those who on her vitals live;
But since that day the war has been
More worthy brave and Christian men.

KLAASZOON'S POWDER MAGAZINE.

A. D. 1606.

Our valiant Rear Admiral, Reiquier Klaaszoon,
All alone, near Cape Vincent, was able to
count
Five galleons approaching, one early fore-
noon,
And each bore more guns than old Klaaszoon could mount.

But his decks are soon cleared for the un-
equal fight:
To their guns his sixty good mariners
stand;
When down bore the Spaniards—that gallant old Knight,
Don Luis de Fasciardo, in command.

" Strike, dog of a Dutchman, that insolent
 flag;
Each officer promptly prepare him to die :
Your sailors to slave in our galleys we'll
 drag ! "
 A broadside was sturdy old Klaaszoon's
 reply.

He fought two long summer days, one
 against five,
 'Till every one living was wounded, on
 board,
And scarce half a score of his men left alive,
 And none but he able to wield pike or
 sword.

" The good ship is sinking, my brave fellows
 all,
 Our last gun is silenced, and struck our
 last blow;
Let us fire our magazine, rather than fall
 In the hands of a hated and triumphing
 foe ! "

A faint cheer replied from the slippery deck,
  Where mangled forms quivered in death's
    agony:
Klaaszoon seized a match—and the stagger-
    ing wreck
  In fragments was strewn on the waves of
    the sea.

Forever remembered, beloved and revered,
  Shall our brave old Admiral's memory be:
His name and his fate to his land are en-
    deared,
  For he died that the land which he loved
    might be free!

DISCOVERY OF THE NIEUW NEDER-LAND BY HENDRICK HUDSON.

A. D. 1609.

O, brave old Hendrick Hudson, bold ex-
plorer of the North!
Through seas beset by storm and ice he
traveled back and forth,
Seeking abroad the fame and gain one's
country oft denies,
He to a foreign land had brought his skill
and enterprise.
At the rich port of Amsterdam the Englishman arrived
Where every risk was ventured and every
venture thrived.
  Brave old Hendrick Hudson!

Our war with cruel Spain, which cost such
floods of blood and tears,
Had been suspended by a truce, to last a
dozen years,

And the Dutch East India Company had
    every effort made,
In many a distant land to seek returns of
    peaceful trade.
So on the Amsterdam Exchange it promptly
    chanced that he
Was hired by the Company again to tempt
    the sea.
      Brave old Hendrick Hudson!

'Twas on the sixth of April, in his yacht, the
    Half Moon good,
He at the Texel squared his sails and to the
    Westward stood,
But half July was gone before his little ves-
    sel lay
In a Gulf of North America, now called Pe-
    nobscot Bay,
And, in view of boastful claims since made,
    it is a trifle odd,
That he was the first of white men who ever
    saw Cape Cod.
      Brave old Hendrick Hudson!

Then, in his saucy little craft, he skirted all
the shore,
And looked upon an empire no man had
found before;
As far as Henlopen and May he ventured to
the South,
And then returning entered a broad river at
its mouth;
He traced the mighty Hudson from its sour-
ces to the sea,
And while its stately current runs his name
shall honored be.
Brave old Hendrick Hudson!

Then hail to Hendrick Hudson, the merry
old sea-dog,
Who never blenched from storm or tide, from
tempest or from fog,
A mariner who trimmed his sails and took
his glass of grog,
And a capital good trencherman at provender
and prog;
As brave and true a seaman as ever kept a log,
And a discoverer who has set old Europe all
agog!
Brave old Hendrick Hudson!

THE BROWNISTS IN HOLLAND.

A. D. 1604—1620.

Some English Brownists—Robinson, Smith,
  Johnson and Ainsworth, and some others—
Set themselves down in Amsterdam,
  And scarce behaved like Christian brothers.
A separatist church they framed,
  An absolutely fresh and new one,
Which, most complacently they claimed,
  Should be the sole correct and true one.

But, falling together by the ears,
  They passed their time in strife and wrang-
    ling,
And scandalized our peaceful Dutch
  With shameful quarrelling and jangling;

For on his brother and his sire
  Johnson laid excommunication,
And doomed them to eternal fire,
  With requisite vituperation.

Ainsworth to Johnson did the same,
  With all formalities required,
Johnson the favor quick returned,
  With a promptness that was much admired.
Vainly our preachers sought to stay
  The fearful war among them raging,
And vainly to our guests did pray
  They'd cease the combat they were waging.

So that their church was scattered; then
  Smith took a new idea surprising,
Became an Anabaptist, and
  Determined upon self-baptizing.
His conscience could not fix on one
  To dip him, so, with all disgusted,
He plunged into a pond alone
  As though none but himself he trusted.

Now Robinson, sole preacher left,
  Hied him to Leyden, where, more rational,
He organized his exile church,
  Which bears the name of Congregational.
But Holland's soil contented not
  These people, nor their bold exhorter,
And Robinson two ships has got
  And they have sailed across the water.

THE ENGLISH PURITANS AT LEYDEN:

A. D. 1620.

These Brownist English exiles who to our
town have come,
Who censure all the rest of us and deem
themselves so pure,
With countenances lengthy and with utter-
ances glum,
Have more peculiar notions than our people can endure.

Because of their Reformed faith we gave
them cordial cheer,
And welcomed every Puritan as fellow,
guest and friend,
But ere they had sojourned with us a quarter
of a year,
We saw that their fault-findings were truly
without end.

They are scandalized extremely by the
music and the dance
In which our youth and children take an
innocent delight,
With direful exclamations and sour looks
askance
They turn away in pious indignation from
the sight.

And they appear, moreover, very much dis-
satisfied
With the way in which we Hollanders ob-
serve the Sabbath day;
And religious toleration, every honest Dutchman's pride,
Is a heresy which they renounce with horror and dismay.

So, 'tis with joy that we have learned they
have permission asked
To settle in Nieuw Nederland, to enjoy
their own belief,
For to keep our patience with them we have
been sorely tasked,
And their departure hence will be a gen-
eral relief.

THE FIELD OF TURNIPS.

A. D. 1628.

A refugee at the Hague was dwelling the
    King of Bohemia,
Welcome enough to the people, quiet and
    fairly respected,
But restless and ill-content with the peace-
    ful life of a citizen,
Crownless, idle and wearing out tedious
    days of exile.

Light lay the fog on the fields, fit for a hunt-
    ing morning,
When to the open country passed the King
    and his hunters,
Down through the even roadways, bordered
    by trees and hedges,
Leaving behind the city, with all its busi-
    ness and bustle.

Slipped from the leash, the hounds sniff on
    the trail of a rabbit,
Horses and riders pell-mell follow the yelp-
    ing chorus,
Fast and furious chase ends in quick disap-
    pointment,
And the pursuit is lost in midst of a field of
    turnips.

Issues from neighboring cottage a stout and
    angry yeoman,
Owner of field and turnips, raises a mighty
    cudgel,
Cries "O King of Bohemia, get thee forth
    from my garden !
Why dost trample the field I had such pains
    in sowing? "

To whom the astonished King made a most
    courteous answer—
" Nay, 'twas these errant hounds led me into
    the trespass.

Surely, unwilling am I to invade the lands of
a freeman.
Sacred to every one should be the fruit of
his labor."

Back, through the even roadways, bordered
with trees and hedges,
Wend they their homeward steps, the royal
hunting procession;
Back to his hired mansion, in the depths of
the city,
Trots the discomfited king, cursing all Dutchmen and turnips.

Anywhere else in Europe, the peasant would
have been punished,
In France he would be sent for life to toil in
the galleys,
And in England his carcase would by the
dogs be eaten:
In Holland he and his turnips thrived 'neath
the law's protection.

"LUCIFER"

(The original of the poem of "Paradise Lost.")

A. D. 1640.

Vondell, the Dutchman, the first of all,
Wrote the tale of the angels' fall;
  Noble his myth and sacred the theme,
Faultless and lofty his measured verse,
  And Sin and Death, in his pious dream,
Descend upon Man as the Demon's curse.

Then, by the Englishman, Milton, was sung
The self-same song in a world-wide tongue,
  And so entrancing the story proved
That Paradise Lost is a household name,
  And men to its faith were strongly moved,
And the grand romance a creed became.

Thus it may chance that a modest word
Is softly uttered and little heard—
  It may to an unknown speech belong,
With purport at first obscurely caught;
  Yet its repetition be bold and strong,
And worlds be filled with an awful thought.

LORD KEEPER FINCH AT THE HAGUE.

A. D. 1641.

An English lord is an exile here,
Escaped from home in a panic of fear.
Well for him that he quickly sped,
For a brief delay would have cost his head:
He managed from London by night to steal,
But he left behind him the King's Great
    Seal.

Tyrant and knave in the day of his power,
He fell from greatness in one brief hour,
Of Parliament's anger he took good heed,
And never stayed to demur or plead.
His pride will gall him, and poverty pinch
The exiled Englishman, Lord Keeper Finch.

GROTIUS.

A. D. 1645.

They brought his body back to Delft
   From the exile land in which he died;
His native town redeemed itself
   By showing forth its tardy pride.
They brought him back beloved of fame,
With many years and a mighty name.

O, madness of these quarrelling creeds,
   Begot of senseless, chattering pride,
By it how oft the patriot bleeds,
   And the philanthropist has died!
Great Grotius it defamed and cursed,
Where now his name is prized and nursed.

THE PEACE OF MUNSTER.

A. D. 1648.

The embassies at last have met,
   The hope of peace at last appears,
Their conference may terminate
   Our long fierce war of eighty years.

Each blow we strike for native land
   Our native land the more endears;
Against the tyrant Spain we stand,
   As we have stood for eighty years.

Each man clings to his native soil,
   Its very name with joy he hears,
But few endure the pain and toil
   Throughout a war of eighty years.

On bloody field and blazing town,
  Men's agony and women's tears,
We've seen the weary suns go down
  Throughout a war of eighty years.

Of all these awful years of fight,
  We've paid them back the long arrears;
With freedom, unity and might,
  We triumph, after eighty years!

DUTCH TOLERATION IN THE SEVEN-TEENTH CENTURY.

To Amsterdam, on one occasion, came
Two foreigners, attracted by its fame,
Florentine merchants they, and strangers
    there,
In search of merchandise unique and rare;
Their errand was to purchase works of art,
Whereof that town the workshop was, and
    mart.

No sooner had they rested at their inn,
Than forth they hied, impatient to begin,
And see those artists whose extended fame
Had reached the distant land from which
    they came;
And they agreed that, first of all, they
    wished
To call upon the painter Vandergrist.

Their greeting o'er, his easels they review,
Praise all his works, and designate a few,
And, after long discourse on art and trade,
The price is settled and the bargain made.
In casual talk the artist somehow saith:
"For me, I am a Calvinist in faith!"

Next, to Melanius they take their way,
And to his labors equal tribute pay;
Again their purses they most gladly ope,
For canvas worthy of a Prince or Pope;
But startle, when by chance this artist man
Complacent, boasts, "I am a Lutheran!"

Van Antwerp next they visit; still they buy;
Van Antwerp says "A Catholic am I!"
They buy of Van Dall, and they almost faint
To learn he is an Anabaptist saint.
They buy of Moses, and—a wonder new!
Moses is undeniably a Jew!

With clanging bells the hour for 'Change
    arrives,
The Italians scamper for their very lives;
Breathless they reach their inn, the door
    they bar,
And tremblingly expect approaching war,
" For, in a town where five religions meet,
There must," say they, "be bloodshed in the
    street! "

They list in vain for sounds of fight or fear,
Then draw the casement and with caution
    peer.
In the broad streets, vast, busy crowds are
    seen,
With friendly gestures and a peaceful mien;
The strangers view the scene with deep sur-
    prise,
Nor find it easy to believe their eyes.

Returned to home, their tale with wonders
    fraught,
Divided interest with the goods they brought;

They told that, 'mongst the Dutch—'twas
    very sad!
Each man a different religion had;
And how those Dutchmen managed to main-
    tain
The peace, was something they could not
    explain!

" MADAME."

A. D. 1670.

Born in a palace, reared near a throne,
Beautiful beyond everything known,
Graceful and gentle, laughing yet shy,
Conquering all with her melting eye,
In her England and France had met,
"Madame" of Orleans, fair Henriette.

What though "Monsieur" be haughty and
     chill,
Morose of temper, infirm of will?
The King himself had royally deigned
To extend to "Madame" a love unfeigned ;
And all night long, as the courtiers know,
They strolled in the woods of Fontainebleau.

Now Louis the aid of Charles would buy,
For he had sworn that Holland should die,
And "Madame" goes, with her witching lips,
To beg of her brother the English ships;
Grand was her progress from court to court;
Peace or War in her hands she brought.

Mutual interest will buy and sell,
Bargains are brief when all goes well,
Louis and Charles became allied friends,
Ruin to Holland their love portends;
But Charles refused, as a thing of course,
To sanction "Madame's" proposed divorce.

Beautiful Henriette homeward hies,
Smiles on her lips, tears in her eyes,
And France is smitten with horror, to see
Her sudden demise in agony.
Venom of poison had caused her death,
Paris whispered it 'neath its breath.

Base Lorraine the poison could send
To avenge " Monsieur " his lord and friend,
And the trembling monarch did not dare
To lay the crime of his brother bare;
'Tis hid, with thousands of guilty things,
In the dark archives of Courts and Kings.

HOW LOUIS XIV. INVADED HOLLAND.

A. D. 1672.

A prey to emotions bitter and dark
He mused in his palace, the *Grand Monarque;*
Not all the delights of his peerless court
Could drive from memory the galling thought
That the feeble folk of a petty State
Had checked his ambition and changed his
    fate.
And His Christian Majesty's anger was lit
At the merest mention of John De Witt,
And, with an outburst of rage, he would
    dwell,
On the harsh treaty of Aix la Chapelle.

And scarce had the ink on that parchment
    dried,
Scarce to their homes had the *diplomats* hied,
When Louis imagined that Holland may
Be as promptly conquered as Franche Comte.

From end to end of his martial realm
He summoned the hosts which should over-
    whelm
The foes who had thwarted his policy,
And drive the Hollanders into the sea!
Horsemen, artillery, footmen, were they,
All drilled by the drill master, Martinet.

Easy for Louis to Europe to show
What an absolute King in his realm can do,
But Charles of England, by Parliament tied,
Was subsidy-seeking on every side:
The best of his fleet, by Dutch enterprise,
Was burned in the Thames before his eyes:
So, his wants unmet, and his pride unhealed,
When Louis for his assistance appealed,
Charles took the new ally, to vex the old,
And their bond of friendship was gold—
    French gold.

Gold, for controlling the English Court,
For with it can lords and courtiers be
    bought;

Gold, for providing the pomp and display,
Wherein his most royal enjoyments lay;
Gold, to remunerate minion and dame,
With guerdons of honor for deeds of shame;
Wrested from starving Frenchmen's toil,
To be spent and squandered on foreign soil;
For peoples must suffer when Kings com-
    bine,
To govern God's footstool by right divine.

Saint George's red banners dance on the sea,
Along with the Bourbonist *fleur de lis*;
The united fleets in the Channel ride,
To bring an end to the Hollanders' pride:
Subjects embrace, who were trained by their
    States,
For hundreds of years, into mutual hates,
And monarchs are banded to trample down
These " burgher folk, who obey no crown."
There were English frigates one hundred
    and ten,
French soldiers two hundred thousand men.

All gaily the Frenchmen crossed our frontier,
In gallant array, in the spring of the year;
Such trains of cannon, an army so great
Had never in Europe invaded a State.
The selected troops of the King's household
Shone brilliant in crimson, and white, and
    gold;
And *fantassin*, light horse and *mousquetaire*,
And body guard, French and Switzer, were
    there;
And their marshals, the first in France were
    they—
Vauban, and Turenne, and the great Conde.

Town after town soon succumbed to its fate,
Yielded submission and opened its gate,
Captains were routed and captains were
    bought,
With never a serious battle fought;
And Yssel and Utrecht and Guelderland
Lay prostrate beneath the invaders' hand:

While greatly the panic and discontent
To the Orange faction new courage lent,
And their partisans shouted in every town,
"Put Orange up and put De Witts down!"

Stained is the record and dark the page
Which tells of that faction's violent rage;
The law was reversed in that desperate hour,
And, selfish and reckless, they seized on
    power.
Both John and Cornelis De Witt had died,
Enshrined in the Fatherland's love and pride;
As patriot freemen they met their fates;
And William, from the reluctant Estates,
The coveted Stadtholdership could wring,
And be, in all but the title, a King.

Meanwhile De Ruyter, in fierce, long fight,
Had put the war fleets of both Kings to
    flight,
And dealt a stern and terrific rebuke
To the insolence of the English Duke;

While the Channel was swept, as in days of
    yore,
And each Dutch ship nailed a broom to the
    fore:
Our rich laden India fleet, home bound,
At the Texel anchored, all safe and sound.
Though few and weak on the land we may be
The Hollanders still were lords of the sea!

But how should our city escape the blow
Aimed by her quickly approaching foe?
That city, Amsterdam, centre of trade,
Where the wealth of the world was stored
    and laid:
The first and chiefest in Europe was she,
The queen of the arts and of industry.
Not higher did the Roman pulses beat
After Lake Thrasymene's dire defeat,
Than the Dutch resolve at that moment rose,
When 'twixt submission and exile they
    chose.

Amsterdam threatened, the crisis was near,
The dykes must be cut, the land disappear,
Leaving the conquering foemen to reign
O'er the seething waves of a watery plain,
And the Holland name would exist no more,
Unless 'twere renewed on some distant shore.
The Farther Indies could furnish a seat
Where a genial clime could the exiles greet;
And the list of intending refugees
Counted fifty thousand full families.

Ho! for this journey of thousands of leagues,
With a welcome peace after war's fatigues,
The tropical seas with their pearls of price,
And the perfumed groves of their isles of
    spice,
And the glowing sun, and the painted skies,
And the balmy airs of a paradise!
Firm in their purpose, the burghers began
To prepare the ships and mature the plan,
That, though old Amsterdam all should be
    lost,
A new one might rise on a fairer coast.

Already Leyden and Delft were submerged,
And the waves o'er the lowlands swirled and
    surged,
When Louis, who came so blithely in May,
Made haste in July to betake him away,
And sought his grand palace of Saint Germain,
Right glad in his heart to be there again;
Leaving his army in sad jeopardy,
Chased and beset by the fast rising sea,
Their camps under water, their finery soiled,
All their campaign and their uniforms
    spoiled.

Ere his Paris Arch of Triumph was done,
All had been lost that King Louis had won,
And the burning a village, or sacking a farm,
Or murdering children, at Swannerdam,
Were all the further exploits in that war,
Which over our borders retreated afar.
And as, in his palace, the *Grand Monarque*
Was nursing his anger, bitter and dark,
Turenne was surrendering each Holland
    town
To " the burgher folk who obey no crown."

THE DYING WORDS OF CORNELIS DE WITT.

A. D. 1673.

Serene in his torments, Cornelis De Witt
Recited the sentiments Horace hath writ—

" Not the wild rush of the popular will,
Not the anger of kings, that can kill,
Not the strong hurricane's howl and dash,
Not the gleam of the lightning's flash
Can shake that man, who, resolved and just,
Has in uprightness reposed his trust."

And Holland remembered the saying when
She needed devoted and resolute men.

A GLASS TO DE RUYTER.

A. D. 1673.

A glass to the memory of Tromp the bold!
  And a glass to the bold De Ruyter!
Since the Vikings roamed the Channel of
    old,
  There has been no such gallant fighter.

Should we strike to the flag of the English
    king?
  Should we cringe to the Stuart's pre-
    tension?
No, rather to sea, and encounter the fleet
  Which he built with the French king's
    pension!

All stranded and fired upon the shore,
  King Charles' ships are consuming,
While one by one, with an impotent roar,
  Their abandoned cannon are booming.

On the Thames, in the sight of London,
  aghast,
  In the sight of their King they are
  burning;
While, with new broom at every topmast,
  De Ruyter is homeward returning.

Then fill to the memory of Tromp the brave!
  And fill to the brave De Ruyter!
And while Orange colors float on the wave,
  Their fame will grow brighter and
  brighter.

SHAFTESBURY IN LONDON AND IN AMSTERDAM.

1. LONDON.—A. D. 1673.

The Earl of Shaftesbury arose, wearing his
    robes and wig,
Lord Chancellor of England, none in Par-
    liament so big,
And freely forth upon the Dutch his noble
    censure poured,
And vented all the enmity with which his
    mind was stored.

"These Hollanders," quoth he, "I rate the
    common enemy
Of all divine-right governments—of every
    monarchy—
Especially our English realm they rival and
    annoy,
' *Delenda est Carthago!*' we must the Dutch
    destroy!"

2. AMSTERDAM.—A. D. 1682.

The Earl has fallen in disgrace, has fled
    from kin and home,
And to our town of Amsterdam, an exile, he
    has come.
He asks our city to protect a helpless
    refugee,
And begs us not to render him unto his
    enemy.

Let all his errors be forgot, and let him
    here abide,
And let us show that tolerance which is our
    nation's pride.
He is welcome to our peaceful town, where
    hostile steps ne'er come ;
Nay, hang his portrait on the wall, beneath
    the stadthuis dome !

BALTHAZAR BEKKER'S "WORLD ENCHANTED."

A. D. 1694.

When witchcraft nonsense was in greatest
    credit,
And Satan's sorceries most deeply dreaded,
(Set forth, at direful length, with brief
    apology,
By James of England, in his "Demonology");
When each beheld his neighbor with sus-
    picion,
Lest he might prove an agent of perdition,
And all with superstitious dread were
    haunted,
Balthazar Bekker wrote his "World En-
    chanted."

He was a man of letters, and of station,
A minister of the Dutch Reformed per-
    suasion;
Not polished nor refined by art or nature—
Ugly as Belzebub in form and feature—

But, with a wealth of Scriptural search and
    learning,
And with a zeal 'gainst fraud and falsehood
    burning,
He wrote his book in Europe's darkest
    hour,
Wherein he dared deny the Devil's power.

The gownsmen of all creeds were deeply
    stirred ;
Rome, Augsburg and Geneva all concurred ;
Each to its clergy was the warning giving,
To kill the Devil would destroy their living.
With all the warmth that interest engen-
    ders,
The Devil's foes appeared as his defenders ;
Of Pastor Bekker's bold attack complained,
And Satan's power to harm mankind main-
    tained.

Condemned by all the ministerial crew
(Though few had patience to peruse it
    through),

His volume was declared to faith opposed,
And Bekker by his synod was deposed.
Lengthy it is, and writ in tiresome prose,
Pedantic was the author and verbose,
But that he dared condemn the "witch-
    craft" craze
Commends his name in more enlightened
    days.

BAAS PIETER IN HOLLAND.

A. D. 1697.

Czar Peter of Russia to Saardam came—
Not as an idler, not as a King,
But as an artisan, learning a trade,
To work in the shipyard, the shop and the
  forge,
To learn how vessels are builded and sailed,
To learn how iron is hammered and cast,
To learn how spars and rigging are trimmed,
To learn how cordage is twisted and wove,
To learn how sails are shifted and spread,
To learn how rudders are worked and hung,
To learn how compass and sextant are used,
To learn how cargoes are loaded and
  shipped,
To learn how Holland has drawn her
  wealth,
And floated her flag upon every sea.

This brawny man with the keen blue eye,
The giant hand and the iron frame,
Labored each day for the workman's wage,
Pored over books at the noonday hour,
Rested at night on a workman's couch,
And, when the Sunday holiday came,
Kept, with his fellows, a wild carouse.
Not disguising his station and rank,
But sharing freely the artisan's life;
Known to his comrades as Pieter de Baas,
Always their equal in workshop or games.
So did he compass the knowledge he sought.
Parted he thence, to return to his realm,
To found an Empire and shapen a State,
To civilize wandering and savage hordes,
Soften the manners and habits of men,
Build up a power colossal in height,
And make his Russia the terror of earth.

TORCY AT THE HAGUE.

A. D. 1790.

The Pensioner Hensius from Holland went
  To plead with Louis for the Orange right,
But not to him the royal brow unbent,
  Nor deigned the King an answer to indite.
"Mercy for thine own subjects," Hensius
    asked,
  But naught obtained he by that strong
    appeal,
Though all his lore and eloquence he
    tasked;
  Louvois e'en threatened him with the
    Bastile!

Years passed, in which the French King,
    vain and mad,
  Had covered Europe with his martial
    dead,
For Fortune was his foe, and stern and sad
  Blow after blow had fallen on his head;

And his young Princes all were in the grave,
  And profligate corruption cursed his
    Court;
Louvois was gone: to France, though fierce
    and brave,
  Each coming day still fresh reverses
    brought.

And Holland was his unrelenting foe,
  Eugene and Marlborough had served her
    well,
Never had insolence been brought so low
  Nor history had such swift revenge to tell.
And now, to Pensioner Hensius, in the
    gloom
  Of evening, at the Hague, the name was
    brought
Of one who waited in his ante-room:
  'Twas Torcy, who an interview had sought.

His armies lost, and squandered all his
    wealth,
  Louis was seized with overpowering
    fright,

And Torcy, leaving scared Versailles by
    stealth,
  Had crossed the frontiers secretly by
    night,
To beg peace from the Burgher Man of
    State—
  Once spurned, insulted, placid through-
    out all—
To crave forgetfulness for pride and hate :
  Did ever a Grand Monarch have such
    fall?

LEGENDS

OF

MANHATTAN ISLAND.

THE ONE-MAN POWER IN NEW AMSTERDAM.

A. D. 1641.

In the good days of old New York
   Her freedom was no sham,
For freedom-loving were the Dutch
   Who built New Amsterdam ;
And when, in sixteen-forty-one,
   An Indian war broke out,
The people clamored to elect
   Their Schepens and their Schout.

At first the Dutch Director, Kieft,
   (Who was Governor, or Mayor,)
By the " better element " controlled,
   Refused their earnest prayer.
Such and so resolute the men
   Who lived here in that day,
That straightway they determined
   No further tax to pay.

When Kieft perceived no way to win,
  By force, or craft, or wit,
He laid his one-man power aside,
  And hastened to submit.
And the freemen of New Amsterdam
  Elected their "Twelve Men,"
As the immemorial usage
  In the Netherlands had been.

And that first City Council,
  Which was chosen in that way,
Is a pattern for self-government
  Down to the present day.
Long the Director strove for power,
  And to put the people down,
Yet "Eight Men," then " Nine Men,"
  Were chosen from the town.

An arbitrary one-man power
  The Dutch would not concede,
And their patriot example
  With us should strongly plead ;

For this sound precept then was taught,
   That justice may be done,
If power be held by many men,
   But not, if given to one.

HOW THE YANKEES TRADED TO THE DELAWARE.

A. D. 1642.

One Lamberton, New Haven man,
  Contrived the Dutch some harm ;
He was a godly Puritan
  As ever sang a psalm.

A vessel full of Yankee goods
  To the Delaware he sent,
For the glory of the Lord—and his
  Own special betterment.

And when the valiant Willem Kieft,
  The Dutch Director here,
Advised him not to traffic there,
  But somewhere else to steer ;

Because the great South River was
  By Dutchmen long possessed,
Who would not brook a rival,
  Though they'd welcome any guest ;

The captain, Herrick, swore to do
  As our Director bade,
And to make mere friendly visit,
  With no intent to trade.

But when he reached the Delaware
  He landed at Hog's Creek,
And having broken cargo,
  Began for trade to seek.

The Yankees made the red man drunk,
  And bought his pelts and skins,
They gave him little wampum, but
  They told him of his sins.

Predestination and free will,
  Foreknowledge and free grace,
They preached to him, and made him
  Dumbfounded for a space.

While he was told his sins were great,
  His income proved but small;
He got a stock of doctrine,
  But that was almost all.

Their exhortations puzzled him,
   Their hymns were loud and long,
And the benighted savage sold
   His peltries for a song.

And now in wrath the Dutch came down,
   And scattered store and post,
And brought this Herrick and his furs
   To the North River coast.

Next caught they pious Lamberton,
   The author of the raid,
And fined him the amount of all
   The profits he had made.

These went their way, declaring
   They never had seen such
An irreligious people
   As they found these Holland Dutch !

PEACE WITH VIRGINIA FORBIDDEN.

A. D. 1660.

Virginia and Nieuw Netherland
   A friendly treaty made
That their respective people
   Might have liberty of trade,
And that all courts of justice,
   In adjudging law and fact,
Between the Dutch and English,
   Be impartial and exact.

But though Stuyvesant and Berkeley
   Agreed that strife should cease,
Yet the stupid laws of Britain
   Have forbid to keep the peace;
And Charles, the King, a warning,
   To his colonies has sent:
"Treaties and laws are only made
   By King and Parliament."

THE CAPTURE OF NIEUW AMSTERDAM.

A. D. 1690.

It was in the month of August
   In sixteen sixty-four,
Four mighty ships of war appeared
   Off Staaten Island shore.
The hateful flag of England
   Flew from their Admiral's mast,
And their cannon, from the port-holes,
   Sent forth a thunderous blast.

Then from each tile-roofed dwelling,
   And from each narrow street,
Came pouring forth our people,
   To view the stranger fleet;
The shopman left his counter,
   The wife her kitchen fire,
And the children left their playground
   To tremble and admire.

The Kings throughout old Europe
   Had sworn to sheathe the sword,
Though well the Dutch Republic knew
   How faithless is their word.
The Kings throughout old Europe
   Have never ceased to hate
The freedom and the tolerance
   Of the Batavian State.

And Charles, the King of England,
   Was hired by the French,
And Louis of France was plotting
   Europe with blood to drench ;
And to the Duke, his brother,
   (Who now has lost his crown,)
The reckless Charles had given
   Our colony and town.

Ours was a prosperous settlement—
   Our stadt huis has the proofs—
Nearly two thousand people,
   Nearly five hundred roofs ;

And, on a Sunday afternoon,
  Gay was the festive scene,
'Neath the walls of old Fort Amsterdam
  And on the Bowling Green.

Our trials and our triumphs
  Had made us proud and free ;
Our town school was already taught,
  And we loved liberty ;
And 'round our hearths brave tales were told
  When evening fires were lit,
Of Civilis and of Barneveldt,
  And Grotius and De Witt.

But the Dutch West India Company
  Had played the tyrant here,
And had denied the equal rights
  To freeborn men so dear ;
And Stuyvesant, their governor,
  His privilege abused,
To enforce the laws and taxes
  Which freeborn men refused.

And so there was a deep resolve,
　　Among both rich and poor,
That anything were better
　　Than that this should endure ;
And on this summer morning
　　Affairs were in such plight,
While Stuyvesant was pondering—
　　Capitulate or fight?

Now was our doughty Governor
　　Determined to resist,
And he smote the Council-table
　　With his dictatorial fist :—
"Ho! man our fort's defenses,
　　And man our city wall,
For never shall Nieuw Amsterdam,
　　Without a battle, fall ! "

But our sagacious burghers,
　　The fathers of the town,
Maintained that his impotent fire
　　Would bring bombardment down.

"Upon our homes and families,
　　Now here without defense,
Your harmless volleys would invite
　　Revengeful violence!

"The good ship 'Gideon' lies astream,
　　And a determined band
Will leave these forfeited domains
　　And sail for Fatherland!
Those who remain have seen their rights
　　Denied and reft away,
And need now fear no harsher rule
　　Beneath the English sway!"

The Governor looked to seaward,
　　At the ships of the English Duke,
He looked upon his people,
　　And heard their bold rebuke;
Heart-broken and despairing
　　And with an oath and frown,
He dashed away a manly tear,
　　And hauled his colors down.

Woe for the flag of Orange,
  That had humbled England's pomp,
When from the seas her fleets were driven,
  By Admiral Van Tromp!
Woe to the sorrowing city,
  Whose choice could only be
Between a foreign conquest
  And a home tyranny!

And woe, too, to that royal Duke
  Who did this treacherous deed,
In exile now he eats his bread—
  The lesson all may read!
A quarter of a century
  Has since passed o'er our town;
We shall regain our liberties,
  But never he his crown!

For, to Dutch as well as English,
  The future is to bring
A century of struggles with
  The Governors of the King;
And when the good time cometh
  For kingly rule to fall,
We Dutch will stand for liberty
  With the foremost of them all!

A LEGEND OF HELL GATE.

A. D. 1675.

A saucy boat was the Annetje Block,
    Periauga-built was the craft ;
She carried at masthead a crowing cock,
    And an Orange streamer abaft.
Her gay young skipper was Hans van Loon,
    From the Wallabout shore he hailed,
And all eyes followed his bounding boat
    As up the East River she sailed.

Who was there, among the Breukelen girls,
    As fair as Lisbet van Pelt,
With her blooming cheeks and her yellow
    curls,
    And her waist in a wampum belt?
With her lover, Hans, she fled from her
    home,
    And they gained the river's side,
Where the Annetje Block, with her streamers
    set,
    Swung on the restless tide.

With the southerly breeze that briskly blew,
  Up the East River they bore,
Past Gouanes Kill and Point Bellevue,
  And the rocky Manhattan shore;
But a squall swooped down on the dancing
    boat,
  And the whirlpool raged about;
You may see the reef where they met their
    death,
  When the Hell Gate tide is out.

THE FIRST EMIGRANTS FROM NEW ENGLAND.

A. D. 1692–1697.

Escaped from New England, they flock to
  our shore,
All jail-worn and wasted, all quaking and
  sore ;
Escaped from the doom of the stake and the
  cord—
Poor victims of that most lamentable fraud,
Which revels in murder, delusion and cant,
Hysteric possessions and clerical rant ;
The shame of the land and reproach of the
  time,
And fills all New England with horror and
  crime !
Yes, these are the "witches!" The Mathers
  maintain
That Satan at Salem has set up his reign ;

Where vicious young women, bewitched, fall
in fits,

And fright judge and jurymen out of their
wits;

While malice and envy, and neighborhood
hate,

Drag down the accused ones, by scores, to
their fate.

'Tis a crime to be old, to be odd, to be poor,

And to own a black cat will conviction
ensure;

'Tis a crime to have gossips, a crime to have
none,

'Tis the greatest of crimes "stated preach-
ing" to shun,

For, woe to the reprobate, mighty or small,

Who under the ministers' censure may fall!

Now, here have we young Philip English
and wife,

Who left lands and ships, and who fled with
bare life.

A neighbor sued English, and when the suit
failed,

On charges of sorcery his sick wife was
jailed.

At Boston, in Arnold's dark prison she lay,
And counted the time till the dread trial
day.
By some friendly aid to New York they
were brought,
And find here the refuge and safety they
sought.
Nathaniel Carey and wife, too, are here;
The wife was imprisoned at Cambridge, last
year.
Her trial for witchcraft at Salem was set,
They fled, and New York's kindly shelter
have met:
He has wife and has freedom, and little he
recks
That his goods are sequestered in old Mid-
dlesex.
And here, too, are Mistress Benom and her
child,
Alleged to have been by the Devil beguiled;
At Hartford once tried, and acquitted, and
then
Through clerical outcry imprisoned again.

Enough, they are safe, for New York's not
    afraid
Of the dire enchantments of matron or maid.

Time comes, when the sons of New England
    shall seek
Of their neighbor Manhattan's great wealth
    to partake ;
Where, with modified zeal, the fierce Puritan
    race
Shall strive, not for creed, but for greed and
    for place ;
When Stoughtons, and Sewells, and
    Cheevers, and Hales,
And other high priests of the gallows and
    jails,
Shall be pastors and masters in pulpit and
    court,
Where our laws are defined or religion is
    taught.
As the young and ambitious abandon her
    shores
And escape, by their flight, her intolerant
    laws,

New York will receive them ; for welcome
to all
Will be ever her greeting to great and to
small ;
Recalling, as honors and favors she grants,
The "witches" who came as their first
emigrants.

EVACUATION DAY BALLAD.

25TH NOVEMBER, A. D. 1783.

Unmenaced now by Foreign Sword,
    But breathing Freedom's native Air,
Let us, with patriot Accord,
    Meet Washington at Chatham Square.

He comes from upper Hudson's banks,
    Through Harlem Heights and Bowerie—
Let him receive the Heartfelt Thanks
    Of those whom he has rendered Free.

He brings us Rescue, Rest and Peace;
    Our long lost Freedom animates;
Compels King George his War to cease
    And recognise our thirteen States.

Our Tyrants hurry to their Ships;
    (They'd burn the Town if they but durst!)
With frenzied oaths and stuttering lips
    They leave the land they long have
    cursed.

Ye Patriots, now in happy rest,
   Look from your Realms of Heavenly
     Bliss,
Leister, Van Dam and Zenger, blest
   To witness such a Day as this!

We'll form a mighty cavalcade;
   Each Son of Liberty be there;
And be our welcome greetings paid
   To Washington at Chatham Square!

NEW YORK'S FIRST DOCTOR.

A. D. 1787.

" As you ride up the road to the Bouwerie,
　But a little piece beyond Bayard's hill,
A clump of towering elms you will see
　Across the way from Delancey's mill ;
Where a peaked roof holds a creaking vane,
　Half hid by the boughs that interlace,
And the traveler looks up a leafy lane
　　And is told, 'tis "old Doctor Tucker's
　　place."

So reads a letter, yellow and old,
　Writ by a hand that has long been dust,
And we only know, as tradition has told,
　　That the grave old doctor was kind and
　　just.
When the fever-stricken rebels lay
　Dying in Sugar House Prison, 'tis said,
The quaint old doctor, by night and day,
　　Had tended the dying and buried the
　　dead.

At the King's College, in fifty-three,
    Back where its graduates' records begin,
He was the first to take the degree
    Which made him Doctor of Medicine.
The street now known as Elizabeth
    Bounded the farm near the Bouwerie
        pike,
Which fell to the doctor upon the death
    Of his mother, Elizabeth Wortendyke.

'Midst his stately elms they ran a street
        through,
    His mulberries gave to another its name,
And the road to his spring, which the whole
        town knew,
    By time and usage Spring Street became.
Near the spot where the old cathedral
        stands,
    He ended in peace his mortal race,
And the mighty city swarms o'er the lands,
    Which once were "old Doctor Tucker's
        place."

THE OLD BREVOORT FARM.

A. D. 1800.

A snug little farm was the Old Brevoort,
Where cabbages grew of the choicest sort;
Full-headed and generous, ample and fat,
In a queenly way on their stems they sat;
And there was boast of their genuine breed,
For from Old Utrecht had come their seed.

These cabbages, made into sauer kraut,
Were the pride of the country round about,
And their flavor was praised at each farmer
    feast,
Among the Stuyvesants, far to the East,
Delanceys, that in the South meadows lay,
And Strykers, perched up at Stryker's Bay.

The Brevoorts had lived, as the record ap-
    pears,
On the farm for almost a hundred years.

From Brevoort in Holland at first they
  came,
From that parent village they took their
  name ;
Whence the head of the family—his name,
  was Rip—
To New Netherlands came in an Amsterdam
  ship.

The farm itself was by no means great
Alongside the Stuyvesants' splendid estate,
But its pumpkins were golden, its apples
  round,
And buckwheat grew on its upland ground ;
For a rule of diet the family had—
To eat buckwheat cakes from green-corn to
  shad.

Some mulberries, quinces and Dordrecht
  pears
Grew where Grace Church its new steeple
  rears ;

Some creeping grape vines on trellis had
    run
Where beckons the statue of Washington;
On the spot where Brevoort House proudly
    towers
Were clumps of orange-hued *bloempje*
    flowers.

The homestead stood at the end of the lands
Where Grace Memorial House now stands;
In its garden, Dutch tulips of every shade,
Their beautiful form and color displayed:
A low-roofed and unpretentious abode,
The homestead confronted a dusty road.

A merry old Dutchman was Uncle Brevoort,
Who had not lived eighty odd years for
    naught;
With abundant waist and laughing blue eye,
And nose of a color a trifle high,
A gouty foot, and long silvery hair,
And a forehead free as a child's from care.

You saw, just through his half-opened door,
The well-scoured planks of a sanded floor;
And within the cupboard was ranged on a
    shelf
Old-fashioned crockery brought from Delft.
The roof o'er his porch for shade was a
    boon
In the heat of a summer afternoon.

In front of the spot where his tulips grew
Ran the road now known as Fourth Avenue;
Thence a lane to East River, through fields
    of wheat,
It now goes by the name of Eleventh Street.
And as the old gentleman sat in his porch
He looked down the lane to the Bouwerie
    Church.

To him, thus enjoying his leisure and cheer,
One fine afternoon, some surveyors drew
    near;
He offered a glass of old Holland schnapps
They accepted with thanks, but produced
    him some maps,

Which showed that a project was well under
    way
To open Eleventh Street through, to Broad-
    way.

The red lines and blue they duly explained,
The land this one owned, the bounds that
    one claimed;
An assessment put here and there an award,
To run curb and gutter through garden and
    sward.
He listened in patience as long as he could,
And then he remarked " he'd be blanked if
    they should ! "

He fought all their maps, and he fought
    their reports,
Corporation, surveyors, commissioners,
    courts;
He hired his lawyers, well learned in the
    law;
The plans and the projects to fragments
    they tore.

But Uncle Brevoort, ere the law suit,
  expires,
And calmly he sleeps at St. Mark's with his
  sires.

The city abandoned the contest at last;
He knew not his triumph, his struggle was
  past
His cabbage plot's built on, his tulips are
  gone,
Where his old homestead stood is a palace
  of stone.
But this of the old Dutchman's pluck we
  can say—
Eleventh Street's not opened through, to
  this day !

NOTES.

Legends of the Netherlands.

Page 1. THE TECTOSAGES.—See Michelet's History of France, Volume 1, Chapter 1, for the extraordinary wanderings of the Tectosages.

Page 4. CIVILIS STANDING ON THE BROKEN BRIDGE.—Tacitus (History, Book v., Chapter xxvi.) relates the revolt of the Batavians under Civilis. These inhabited the country now called Holland. A parley is asked by the Roman Consul Cerealis. The two leaders meet to confer, upon a broken bridge. Here the manuscript of Tacitus is torn ; the rest of the tale is lost, and we know not the result of the conference, or of the rebellion.

Page 13. Ritterband.—Free Lances.

Page 18. Haarlem is a contraction of *Heer Lem*, "Lord William."

Page 19. THE COUNTESS JANE.—The common people believed that Count Baudouine returned from the East, and was put to death by his daughter.

Page 32. "With them died Knighthood."—Seventeen of the Knights were of Flanders.

Page 36. MAESTRICHT.—The sovereignty of Maestricht could only be exercised by the joint action of the Bishop and Duke. This situation gave rise to many satirical and popular ballads.

Page 47. HOW BURGUNDY GOT LUXEMBOURG.—"Repondit que oui, que le Duc estoit d'aultre metail, car il l'avoit gardé, porté et soutenu."

Page 66. "That his family madness came to view." —The Emperor's mother was insane, and his own contemporaries believed him to have been, when he resigned the imperial crown at the age of 56, and retired to the Convent of St. Just.

Page 69. "These are but as beggars"—*De Geuzen*.

Page 75. "For the spy and poisoner obey me."— The poisoning of Don Juan followed Philip's discovery of his secret treaty with Elizabeth.

Page 76. Schepen : Esquire or City Sergeant. Stadthuis : City Hall.

Page 88. QUEEN ELIZABETH ARRAIGNED.—Elizabeth insulted the Dutch Ambassadors on the very eve of the sailing of the Great Spanish Armada.

Page 101. "A Gulf of North America."—The Dutch writers denied Gosnold's alleged discovery in 1602.

Page 103. THE BROWNISTS IN HOLLAND.—See Neal's History of the Puritans, Part II., chapter 1.

Page 107. "Permission Asked to Settle in Nieuw Nederland."—The States-General refused this application, but the King of England then gave them permission to sail for New England.

Page 108. THE FIELD OF TURNIPS.—This story is related by Michelet.

Page 114. THE PEACE OF MUNSTER.—The rebellion of the Netherlands lasted eighty-two years—from the signing of the petition for Religious Freedom, 10th February, 1596, to the acknowledgement of Dutch Independence by the King of Spain by the Treaty of Munster, 15th May, 1648.

Page 116. DUTCH TOLERATION IN THE 17TH CENTURY.—This story is told by Voltaire.

Page 120. "MADAME"—Wife of the Duke of Orleans and sister of Charles II. of England.

Page 121. "Venom of poison caused her death."—It was then so believed, but late writers, as M. Miguet, have maintained that "Madame" died of an intestinal inflammation.

Page 131. "The Sentiments Horace hath Writ."—See Horace, ode 3, book 3.

Page 132. "Fired Upon the Shore."—The burning of the English fleet in the Thames is not a favorite subject for English historians.

Page 136. "WORLD ENCHANTED." — "Betooverde Wereld.

Page 138. BAAS PIETER.—While the Czar sojourned at Saardam, he led the life of a common workman, although his name and rank were known to his employers and to many of his associates.

Page 141. Torcy was Louis XIV.'s Minister of Foreign Affairs.

Legends of Manhattan Island.

Page 154. THE CAPTURE OF NIEUW AMSTERDAM.— This is the narrative as told among the Dutch people of New York, in the time of Governor Jacob Leisler, about A. D. 1690.

Page 162. THE FIRST EMIGRANTS FROM NEW ENGLAND.—Many persons accused of witchcraft fled in these years from New England to New York, where they were received and protected. These remarks are supposed to be addressed by one New Yorker to another, perhaps during a walk by the river side, or on the battery.

Page 162. "The Mathers."—Clergymen who insti-
gated prosecutions for so-called withcraft in New
England.

Page 165. "Stoughtons, and Sewells, and Cheevers
and Hales."—Prosecutors of witches in Massa-
chusetts.

Page 167. EVACUATION DAY BALLAD.—As supposed
to have been sung by New Yorkers on the day of
the British evacuation of their city, on the 25th
of November, 1783.

Page 169. NEW YORK'S FIRST DOCTOR.—The first
physician graduated in America was Dr. Robert
Tucker, of New York City, who received his
degree of M. D. at King's (now Columbia) College
in 1753.

Page 170. "They ran a street": Elm Street.

Page 170. "Mulberries gave to another its name";
Mulberry Street.

CONTENTS.

Legends of the Netherlands.

		PAGE
The Tectosages . . . . B. C. 300		I
Civilis Standing on the Broken Bridge A. D. 70		4
Augustus Carausius 250		7
Friesland and Zeeland 850		11
How the Bishop Saved Utrecht 1137		12
Count Willem's Crusade 1218		15
The Countess Jane 1223		19
Guy Dampierre and His Daughter . . . 1300		21
The Cods and the Hooks 1300–1500		23
The Battle of Courtrai 1302		25
The Burning Alive of the Knights Templars 1314		29
The Exile of Peter Du Bois from Ghent . 1386		34
The Lords of Maestricht 1400		36
How Arnold Beiling Died 1424		38
The Days of the Dukes of Burgundy . . 1425		40
How Burgundy got Luxembourg 1462		47
Charles of Guelderland 1500		49
Charles Quint in His Cradle 1500		53
The Sixteenth Century Deluge 1524		55
Commissioner Smyter at Hoorn 1550		61

PAGE

The Siege of Metz 1552   65

" Vivent les Gueux ! " 1566   67

The Three Oranges 1568-1647   70

The Rescue of Leyden 1574   72

Philip's Soliloquy on His Brother 1578   75

Song of the Artisans of Antwerp 1580   76

The Spanish Soldier 1580   78

The Fleshers of Antwerp 1584   80

The Tragedy at Delft 1584   83

Gresham's Draft on Genoa 1587   85

Queen Elizabeth Arraigned 1588   88

The Surrender of Deventer 1591   91

Philip's Hatred 1600   93

The Battle of Tiel 1600   94

Klaaszoon's Powder Magazine 1606   97

Discovery of the Nieuw Nederland. . . . 1609   100

The Brownists in Holland 1604-1620   103

The Puritans at Leyden 1620   106

The Field of Turnips 1628   108

"Lucifer," the Original of "Paradise

Lost". 1640   111

Lord Keeper Finch at the Hague 1641   112

Grotius 1645   113

The Peace of Munster 1648   114

Dutch Toleration in the 17th Century . . 1650   116

"Madame" 1670   120

How Louis XVI. Invaded Holland . . . 1672   123

The Dying Words of Cornelius DeWitt · 1672   131

		PAGE
A Glass to De Ruyter ! 1673		132
Shaftesbury in London and in Amsterdam 1673–1682		134
Balthazar Bekker's " World Enchanted " 1694		136
Baas Pieter in Holland 1697		139
Torcy at the Hague 1709		141

Legends of Manhattan Island.

The One-Man Power in Nieuw Amsterdam . . . . A. D. 1641		147
How the Yankees Traded to the Delaware River 1642		150
Peace with Virginia Forbidden 1660		153
The Capture of Nieuw Amsterdam . . . 1664		154
A Legend of Hell Gate 1675		160
The First Emigrants from New England 1692–1697		162
Evacuation Day Ballad of 25th November 1783		167
New York's First Doctor 1787		169
The Old Brevoort Farm 1800		171

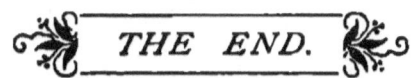

THE END.